U0066890

科技英文寫作系列之五

科技英文編修訓練手冊 進階篇

Advanced Copyediting Practice for Chinese Technical Writers

作者 / 柯泰德 (Ted Knoy)

強力推薦！

國立交通大學校長　張俊彥
… 此書對理工學生及從事科技研究人士相當有用，特推薦之！

工研院院長　史欽泰
… 提供簡單、明白的寫作原則，非常適合科技研發人員使用

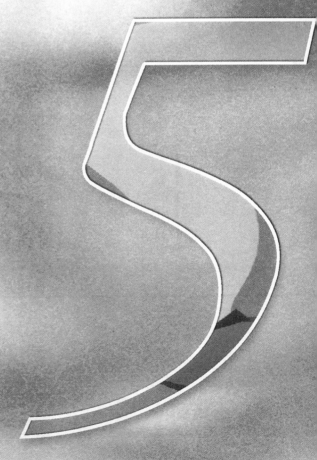

文化 / 科技 / 品質 / 創意 · 清蔚科技出版事業部
四方書網 http://www.4Book.com.tw

Advanced Copyediting Practice for Chinese Technical Writers

科技英文編修訓練手冊—進階篇

By Ted Knoy

柯 泰 德

清蔚科技股份有限公司

Also available in the Chinese Technical Writers Series
（科技英文寫作系列）

An English Style Approach for Chinese Technical Writers
精通科技論文（報告）寫作之捷徑

English Oral Presentations for Chinese Technical Writers
作好英語會議簡報

A Correspondence Manual for Chinese Technical Writers
英文信函參考手冊

An Editing Workbook for Chinese Technical Writers
科技英文編修訓練手冊

Also available in the Chinese Professional Writers Series
應用英文寫作系列

Writing Effective Study Plans
有效撰寫英文讀書計畫

您可以透過以下方式購買

四方書網　http://www.4Book.com.tw
郵政劃撥　帳戶　清蔚科技股份有限公司
　　　　　帳號　19419482
清蔚科技股份有限公司

The book is dedicated to my wife, Hwang, Li-Wen.

序言

　　近年來，台灣科技發展日新月異，突飛猛進，已漸與美日並駕齊驅，居於世界領先地位。然而國內科技人士在國際期刊及學術研討會上發表研究成果時，往往無法將其一流之研究成果確實而清楚的表達出來，讓國際間學者接受。這方面問題鄰近的日本也有相同的困擾，其中的關鍵在於英文寫作能力與語文表達技巧的不足。因此，欲提昇台灣科技研究在國際間的地位，使台灣不僅在技術發展層面領先，更在學術研究上能更上層樓，首先要提昇科技人才在英文語文能力的素養，如此不僅可以迅速吸收國際間頂尖的科技知識，也能將國內的研究成果國際化，促進交流及提昇台灣的國際地位。

　　個人投身於台灣之學術教育與科技研究已過四十寒暑，擔任過三百多位碩士及五十幾位博士學生的論文指導教授，有感於台灣學生或年輕之研發人員在撰寫科技論文或發表研究論文時，常常無法明確清楚地表達出來，尤其英文能力又常是理工學生較弱的一環，這將造成台灣在科技發展上的阻礙。交通大學這幾年在半導體、通訊及資訊系統方面的研究已達世界一流水準，在國際著名期刊發表的論文數更是世界第一，然而在論文寫作技巧與質的提昇上是未來努力的方向。柯老師這幾年來致力於科技英文寫作的教育，並在交大及清大授課，幫助同學在科技論文寫作能力的提昇上，貢獻良多。現在將其豐富經驗撰成此書，對於國內理工學生及從事科技研究之人士而言，可說是一本相當有用的書籍，特向讀者推薦之，並期許台灣朝向學術國際化發展，向前邁進！！

交通大學校長暨中研院院士

張 俊 彥 謹識

2000 年 5 月

名人推薦

蔡仁堅—新竹市長

　　科技不分國界，隨著進入公元兩千年的資訊時代，使用國際語言撰寫學術報告已是時勢所趨；今欣見柯泰德先生致力於編撰此著作，並彙集了許多實例詳加解說，相信對於科技英文的撰寫有著莫大的裨益，特予以推薦。

史欽泰—工研院院長

　　台灣的科技水準日益提昇，國際活動日趨頻繁，明確的英文寫作在國際上適當的表達我國科技研究成果是每個研究工程人員，學者應提升的的能力。　柯君服務於工研院化工所，從平日的工作中對國人英文寫作之毛病知之甚詳，本書即以實用範例，針對國人寫作的缺點提供簡單、明白的寫作原則，非常適合科技研發人員使用。

楊日昌—工研院副院長

　　本書指出幾種英文寫作常犯錯誤，並藉由實際範例及反覆練習訓練讀者寫作清楚正確的英文句子，值得作為提昇英文寫作能力之參考。

許尚華—國立交通大學工業工程與管理系主任

　　學習科技英文寫作技能，不外乎勤讀、勤寫。但是在學寫之時，需要有良師指導。柯泰德先生積其幾年來教授國人科技英文寫作以及協助論文寫作之經驗，編撰此書，內文兼具原則與實例，相信讀者能從其間獲益菲淺。

張智星—國立清華大學資訊工程學系副教授、計算中心組長

　　本書是特別針對系上所開科技英文寫作非同步遠距教學而設計，範圍內容豐富，所列練習也非常實用，學生可以配合課程來使用，在時間上更有彈性的針對自己情況來練習，很有助益。

劉世東—長庚大學醫學院微生物免疫科主任

論文寫作是科學研究者最重要的工作。能夠將英文順利地寫出來，用最精簡的方法，清楚地表達自己的意思，並且在科學邏輯上，語意上，及文法上不犯錯，並不是一件很容易的事。本書的作者在台多年，深知中國人最容易犯的錯，而撰寫這本書。書中的例子及習題對閱讀者會有很大的助益。這是一本研究生必讀的書，也是一般研究者重要的參考書。

周鳳英—清大原科中心同位素組主任

我國之科技人員英文寫作機會甚多，但要將科技英文寫的精確、明白對多數國人來並非容易之事。本書作者萃取其多年英文教學與修編經驗著此書，針對國人寫作之缺點提供清楚之修編實例，讓讀者在短時間內掌握英文寫作之重點，實用性高，極具參考價值。

王文賢—工研院開放實驗室經理

今日身處國際化時代的科技人員，欲圖表達個人專業，"英文"是最直接而鋒利的工具。國人多受挫於外語，尤其是科技專業人員。英文表達有不同於中文者，不只來自於生活經驗，更源於思考的不同。柯泰德先生以其對國人及中文的深入，專精於華人科技英文教學，也在工研院任職修改科技論文多年，頗能一針見血的協助我們。從柯先生保持原稿的修訂方式，我們不只可以發現文字差異，也能學到思考差異間的精髓。

蘇自平—工研院機械所國際業務室經理

本書以捷要的單元及深入的說明含括了深一層的科技寫作精華。單元中的練習內容不僅能提供英文文稿的正確詞句架構而且可作為日常英文寫作的自我更正演練。對於目前正從事國際業務者或躋身於全球電子商務的企業家及科技人員來說，此書可作為排除中英文寫作中易面臨的語法困擾。本人極力推薦此書〝手到〞的實用效益及參考價值。

TABLE of CONTENTS

FOREWORD

Technical writing is an essential tool for garnering international recognition of accomplishments made by Taiwan's technical and scientific community. To meet this need, **The Chinese Technical Writers Series** seeks to provide a sound technical writing curriculum and, on a more practical level, to provide valuable reference guides for Chinese technical and managerial professionals. The Series supports Chinese technical writers in the following areas:

Writing style

The books in this Series seek to transform archaic ways of writing into a more active and direct writing style that makes the author's main ideas easier to identify.

Structure and content

Another issue facing technical writers is how to organize the structure and contents of manuscripts and other common forms of writing. The exercises in this workbook will help writers to avoid and correct stylistic errors commonly found in technical documents.

Quality

Technical writers inevitably prepare manuscripts to meet the expectations of editors, referees/reviewers, as well as to satisfy journal requirements. The books in this Series are prepared with these specific needs in mind.

Advanced Copyediting Practice for Chinese Technical Writers is the fifth book in the Chinese Technical Writers Series.

　　『Advanced Copyediting Practice for Chinese Technical Writers 』爲「科技英文寫作系列（ The Chinese Technical Writers Series）」之第五本書，本手冊中練習題部份主要是幫助科技英文作者避免及糾正常犯寫作格式上錯誤，由反覆練習中，進而熟能生巧提升寫作及編修能力。

「科技英文寫作系列」針對以下內容逐步協助中國人解決在科技英文寫作上所遭遇之各項問題：

A . 寫作型式：把往昔通常習於抄襲的寫作方法轉換成更主動積極的寫作方式，俾使讀者所欲表達的主題意念更加清楚。

B . 方法型式：指出國內寫作者從事英文寫作或英文翻譯時常遇到的文法問題。

C . 內容結構：將科技寫作的內容以下面的方式結構化：工程目標、工程動機、 個人動機。並了解不同的目的和動機可以影響論文的結構，由此，獲得最適當的論文內容。

D . 內容品質：以編輯、審查委員的要求來寫作此一系列之書籍，以滿足期刊的英文要求。

本手冊乃是科技英文寫作系列中第五本著作, 其他尚有
　　1.精通科技論文（ 報告 ）寫作之捷徑
　　2.作好英語會議簡報
　　3.英文信函參考手冊
　　4.科技英文編修訓練手冊

INTRODUCTION

Clarity in technical writing ensures that the intended meaning is not misconstrued. Fully comprehending a manuscript's technical contents requires omitting ambiguity and obscurity. Clarity focuses on allowing the reader to easily understand what the writer is trying to communicate. Restated, clarity eases comprehension.

The previous book in the Chinese Technical Writers Series, <u>An Editing Workbook for Chinese Technical Writers</u>, emphasized revising for **conciseness** so that technical contents are as succinct as possible. An extension of the writing style principles introduced in that book, this advanced copyediting practice workbook stresses revising for **clarity** to ensure that the author's intended meaning is evident.

The exercises in this Workbook are part of the technical writing course offered at the Department of Computer Science, National Tsing Hua University. Further details regarding the course can be found via the World Wide Web at http://mx.nthu.edu.tw/~tedknoy

（ 引導介紹 ）

" 明白寫作 " 原則可使科技英文作者想表達的意思不會被誤解。就是要把文章中的曖昧不清全部去除。" 明白寫作 " 強調如何使您文章的讀者很容易的理解您作品的精髓。

科技英文寫作系列之四 ---" 科技英文編修訓練手冊 " 強調精確寫作， 而本書(進階篇)延續其寫作指導原則，更進一步把重點放在如何讓作者想表達的意思更明顯，即 -- 明白寫作。

本書練習題為國立清華大學資訊工程系非同步遠距教學科技英文寫作課程中之一部份內容，相關課程細節請參閱以下網址：http://mx.nthu.edu.tw/~tedknoy

Copyediting marks used in this Workbook

修改前句子	修改後句子	修改符號的代表意義
Writee for clarity.	Write for clarity.	***Delete*** 刪除
Subject and verb must agree agree.	Subject and verb must agree.	***Insert*** 插入文字
new information Add to a sentence.	Add new information to a sentence.	
Pronouns must have a clear referent.	Pronouns must have a clear referent.	***Insert space*** 插入空格
# Pronouns must have a clear referent.	Pronouns must have a clear referent.	
Videotape	videotape	***Lower case*** 大寫改成小寫
VIDEOTAPE	videotape	
harvard university	Harvard University	***Capitals*** 小寫改成大寫
mit	MIT	
modifier problems Omit	Omit modifier problems.	***Transpose*** 前後對調
in structure and meaning Create sentences parallel	Create sentences parallel in structure and meaning.	
Avoid unnecessary shifts	Avoid unnecessary shifts.	***Period*** 句點

Write for Clarity

單元一：明白寫作

What the author writes often differs from his or her intended meaning. That is, an author's intended meaning is often lost. When editing, clarity is vital so as not to mislead the reader. In addition to writing concise sentences, the reader must be able to fully comprehend the manuscript, thereby ensuring that the paper flows smoothly.

The exercises in this unit test a writer's ability to clarify meaning in a technical document.

科技英文寫作者常常寫非所想，當然誤導了讀者，此時明白寫作就很重要，除了要把文章寫得精確以外，更要使讀者不誤解您的意思。

本單元練習想測試一下您明白寫作的功力。

Exercise 1

Correct the following sentences using the copyediting marks on page 1.

1. The number of banks charging their customers ATM user fees are increasing.

2. The majority of the committee feel that the right decision was made.

3. Time as well as temperature are important during the batch process.

4. The professor told the student that he needed to finish early.

5. The graduate assistant conducted the experiment. Time and the amount of pressure applied to the conductive material were essential to success; however, it lasted too long.

6. Different criteria often conflict with each other, which implies that simultaneously optimizing different objectives is relatively difficult.

7. The Taguchi approach combines experimental design techniques with quality loss considerations and the average quadratic loss is minimized as well.

8. Engineers must either combine all inputs to create the output of a product or the parameter values must be set so that the product's performance remains unaffected.

9. The notions can be simply modified by implementing the following procedure:

Select the levels that maximize SN.

Estimate the slope of the linear regression model.

The control factors and the adjustment factors must be identified.

Identify the control factors that significantly affect the variables.

The target must be adjusted as much as possible.

10.　To simulate the program, precautions must be taken by the engineer.

11.　As a graduate student, my academic advisor gave me much valuable advice.

12.　Before examining all of the available options, the decision was made to initiate the plan.

13.　The proposed procedure corrects dimensional distortion and errors better.

14.　Our company prefers that organization more than their institute.

15.　The new company is as competitive, if not more competitive than, existing ones.

16.　When a student is preparing for an examination, you should get plenty of rest before the test.

17. The professor prefers using a calculator to estimate costs instead of

using a pen because they can more easily add numbers.

18. The graduate student recorded the data and then writes a summary

report.

Answers
Exercise 1

1.　The number of banks charging their customers ATM user fees ~~are~~ *is/g*

increasing.

The number of banks charging their customers ATM user fees is increasing.

EDITOR'S NOTE 1.1 The subject must agree with the verb. *The number of* takes a singular verb while *A number of* takes a plural verb.

2.　The majority of the committee feel *s* that the right decision was made.

The majority of the committee feels that the right decision was made.

EDITOR'S NOTE 1.2 The verb should be singular since the noun *committee* refers to <u>a unit</u> of people. However, consider the following sentence: The majority of notebook computers purchased abroad are made in Taiwan.

In this case, the verb should be plural since the noun refers to <u>individual</u> computers.

3.　Time as well as temperature ~~are~~ *is/g* important during the batch process.

Time as well as temperature is important during the batch process.

> **EDITOR'S NOTE 1.3** Expressions such as *as well as*, *in addition to*, *along with*, *accompanied by* and *with* should not confuse the reader into thinking that the sentence has a compound subject and, therefore, should have a plural verb.

4.   The professor told the student ~~that he~~ needed to finish early.

   "You"

The professor told the student, "You need to finish early."

> **EDITOR'S NOTE 1.4** Unambiguous pronoun references ensure that the reader does not misinterpret the intended meaning. In the original sentence, who needs to finish early (*the professor* or *the student*) is ambiguous because who he refers to is not clear.

5.   The graduate assistant conducted the experiment. ~~T~~ime and the

amount of pressure applied to the conductive material were essential

to success~~;~~ however, ~~it~~ lasted too long.

   Although   *the process*

**The graduate assistant conducted the experiment. Although time and the
amount of pressure applied to the conductive material were essential to
success, the process lasted too long.**

> **EDITOR'S NOTE 1.5** The farther that the pronoun is placed away from its antecedent makes it more difficult for the reader to understand what the pronoun refers to. In the original sentence, *experiment* is the antecedent to which *it* refers. However, the reader may erroneously assume that *time* or *pressure* is the antecedent for *it*. In the revised sentence, instead of repeating *the experiment* twice, *the process* is used to avoid confusion.

6.   Different criteria often conflict with each other, ~~which~~ impl~~ies~~ *ying* that

simultaneously optimizing different objectives is relatively difficult.

Different criteria often conflict with each other, implying that simultaneously optimizing different objectives is relatively difficult.

OR

The fact that different criteria often conflict with each other implies that simultaneously optimizing different objectives is relatively difficult.

OR

Different criteria often conflict with each other; this situation implies that simultaneously optimizing different objectives is relatively difficult.

> *EDITOR'S NOTE 1.6* Avoid the tendency to use *which, this,* and *that* when referring to a previous clause or sentence. Informal English commonly uses this habit, such as in the following sentence: *Saving money is a wise strategy for youth, which is also the characteristic of a thrifty individual.* The problem is that what *which* refers to is unclear: *saving money* or *youth.*

7. The Taguchi approach combines experimental design techniques with quality loss considerations and the average quadratic loss is minimized as well.

   The Taguchi approach combines experimental design techniques with quality loss considerations and minimizes the average quadratic loss as well.

   > *EDITOR'S NOTE 1.7* A sentence must have a parallel structure. Words, phrases or clauses should be in the same grammatical form. In the sentence, with the first part in active voice and the latter part in passive voice, the sentence is not parallel and awkward.

8. Engineers must either combine all inputs to create the output of a product or the parameter values must be set so that the product's performance remains unaffected.

Engineers must either combine all inputs to create the output of a product or set the parameter values so that the product's performance remains unaffected.

EDITOR'S NOTE 1.8 Sentences containing correlative expressions such as *either...or, neither...nor, not only...but also* must be parallel in structure.

9.   The notions can be simply modified by implementing the following procedure:

Select the levels that maximize SN.

Estimate the slope of the linear regression model.

The control factors and the adjustment factors must be identified.

Identify the control factors that significantly affect the variables.

The target must be adjusted as much as possible.

The notions can be simply modified by implementing the following procedure:

Select the levels that maximize SN.

Estimate the slope of the linear regression model.

Identify the control factors and the adjustment factors.

Identify the control factors that significantly affect the variables.

Adjust the target as much as possible.

> **EDITOR'S NOTE 1.9** A sentence containing a list must be parallel in structure.

10. To simulate the program, precautions must be taken by the engineer.

To simulate the program, the engineer must take precautions.

OR

The engineer must take precautions when simulating the program.

> **EDITOR'S NOTE 1.10** Although the writer intended to state that *the engineer* is simulating the program, the modifier in front of the sentence *To simulate the program,* does not logically modify *the engineer.* This is known as a dangling modifier.

11. *when I was* As a graduate student, my academic advisor gave me much valuable advice.

My academic advisor gave me much valuable advice when I was a graduate student.

> **EDITOR'S NOTE 1.11** Similar to the dangling modifier in the previous sentence, the clause *As a graduate student* mistakenly implies the subject of the sentence *my academic advisor.*

12. Before examining all of the available options, the decision was made

to initiate the plan.

Before examining all of the available options, they decided to initiate the plan.

Or even better

They decided to initiate the plan before examining all of the available options.

13. The proposed procedure corrects dimensional distortion and errors

betterx   *than conventional options.*

The proposed procedure corrects dimensional distortion and errors better

than conventional options.

> **EDITOR'S NOTE 1.12** The comparison is incomplete in this sentence. *The proposed procedure corrects dimensional distortion and errors better* than what? Both items that are compared must be stated, not just implied.

14. Our company prefers that organization more than their institute   *does.*

Our company prefers that organization more than their institute does.

OR

Our company prefers that organization more than we prefer their institute.

> **EDITOR'S NOTE 1.13** What is being compared is unclear in this sentence. Depending on the writer's intended meaning, the revised sentence eliminates this confusion.

15. The new company is as competitive *as*, if not more competitive than, existing ones.

The new company is as competitive as, if not more competitive than, existing ones.

> ***EDITOR'S NOTE 1.14*** The second *as* must always be used when using comparative expressions such as *as strong as* and *as good as*.

16. When a student is preparing for an examination, *he or she* should get plenty of rest before the test.

When a student is preparing for an examination, he or she should get plenty of rest before the test.

Or even better

When preparing for an examination, a student should get plenty of rest before the test.

> ***EDITOR'S NOTE 1.15*** The writer should avoid shifting from Third Person to First Person, or vice versa. The writer should also avoid shifting from First Person to Second Person.
>
> Consider the following example:
>
> > **Original**
> > **I will not go to a coffee shop where you can not use the shop's electrical outlet for your notebook computer.**
> >
> > **Revised**
> > **I will not go to a coffee shop where I can not use the shop's electrical outlet for my notebook computer.**

17. The professor prefers using a calculator to estimate costs instead of
     using a pen because ~~they~~ *it / gr* can more easily add numbers.

The professor prefers using a calculator to estimate costs instead of using a pen because it can more easily add numbers.

> ***EDITOR'S NOTE 1.16*** The writer should not shift the number that is attributed to the pronoun.

18. The graduate student recorded the data and then ~~writes~~ *wrote / gr* a summary
     report.

The graduate student recorded the data and then wrote a summary report.

> ***EDITOR'S NOTE 1.17*** Shifting verb tense in a sentence is undesirable. However, a shift in verb tense is acceptable if the writer refers to something that occurred in the past, but then states a fact, finding, observation or assumption based on this previous event.
>
> Consider the following example:
>
> Tsai and Li [2] ***examined*** the factors that influence thermal stability, indicating that temperature ***plays*** a prominent role.
>
> However, this example is the exception rather than the rule. Avoid unnecessary shifts in verb tense.

Exercise 2

Correct the following sentences using the copyediting marks on page 1.

1. Either the supply or consumers determines the market outcome.

2. The department chairman and professor are my current employer.

3. Telecommunications have been widely studied in recent years.

4. The optimization phase determines a feasible factor level combination to optimize the process quality. This may be difficult for users without previous statistical training.

5. After the board meeting was finished, they left the room.

6. It is preferred in standard methods to select a tentative model based on censored data.

7. This study focuses on examination of Taguchi's two step procedure and demonstrating how the wafer quality is improved in the deposition process.

8. The two step procedure attempts to identify those factors that significantly affect the signal-to-noise (SN) ratio and finding the adjustment factors that markedly influence the mean.

9. The adjustment factors are found by selection of the appropriate levels and to vary the surrounding factors.

10. Being a volatile compound, the chemist handled the mixture with extreme caution.

11. The new computer has many improved functions that reached the market last week.

12.   The modem offered by the manufacturer with the latest functions has many advantages over older models.

13.   The input's power is greater than the output.

14.   The back propagation network can be used estimate the mapping function between the two variables.

15.   The novel algorithm is more efficient in terms of computational cost.

16.   Turn on the machine and the valve should be closed.

17.   The academic advisor asked the graduate student if the paper was completed and is it ready to send to the journal for review?

18.   The laboratory manager arranged the meeting and the discussion was led by him.

Answers

Exercise 2

1.   Either the supply or consumers determines *[gl]* the market outcome.

Either the supply or consumers determine the market outcome.

> ***EDITOR'S NOTE 1.18*** Whenever *or* or *nor* connects two subjects, the subject closest to the verb should determine whether the verb is singular or plural. Since ***consumers*** is the closest to the verb, the verb should be plural.

2.   The department chairman and professor ~~are~~ *is/gl* my current employer.

The department chairman and professor is my current employer.

Or even better

The professor who acts as the chairman is my current employer.

> ***EDITOR'S NOTE 1.19*** Although a plural verb is usually used when two or more subjects are connected by ***and***, a singular verb should be used when the two or more subjects refer to the same person or thing.

3.   Telecommunications ~~have~~ *has/gl* been widely studied in recent years.

Telecommunications has been widely studied in recent years.

> ***EDITOR'S NOTE 1.20*** Because a noun is plural in form (ending in *s* or *es*) does not mean that it is plural in meaning. Like ***telecommunications***, other examples such as ***mathematics, physics*** and ***economics*** take singular verbs because they refer to a single body of knowledge.

4.   The optimization phase determines a feasible factor level combination

approach)

to optimize the process quality. This ~~may~~ be difficult for users

without previous statistical training.

The optimization phase determines a feasible factor level combination to optimize the process quality. This approach may be difficult for users without previous statistical training.

EDITOR'S NOTE 1.21 Beginning a sentence with **This** or **That** may confuse the reader as to what the writer is referring to. In this sentence, the reader could confuse **This** to refer to only **optimization phase**, **feasible factor level combination** or **process quality**. Instead, adding **approach** behind **This** lets the reader know what the author is referring to in the previous sentence.

participants)

5.   After the board meeting was finished, they left the room.

After the board meeting was finished, the participants left the room.

Or even better

The participants left the room after the board meeting was finished.

EDITOR'S NOTE 1.22 A writer occasionally uses a pronoun to imply what it refers to, thereby assuming that the reader will know what the referent for the pronoun is. However, some readers do not understand what the writer is implying when a pronoun is used. Since the **board meeting** is made up of participants, the writer used the pronoun **they**, assuming that the reader would understand. However, this implied meaning often creates confusion.

ing

6.   ~~It is preferred in~~ standard methods ~~to~~ select a tentative model based on

censored data.

Standard methods prefer selecting a tentative model based on censored data.

> **EDITOR'S NOTE 1.23** Spoken English often uses **they, it,** and **you** without a particular referent in mind. For example **"In Taiwan, they use chopsticks."** However, in writing, **they, it,** and **you** should not be used unless they have an antecedent.

7.   This study ~~focuses on~~ examination of Taguchi's two step procedure and demonstrating how the wafer quality is improved in the the/ deposition process.

This study examines Taguchi's two step procedure and demonstrates how the deposition process improves the wafer quality.

> **EDITOR'S NOTE 1.24** A sentence is not parallel when a noun **(examination)** and a gerund **(demonstrating)** are used together.

8.   The two step procedure attempts to identify those factors that significantly affect the signal-to-noise (SN) ratio and finding the adjustment factors that markedly influence the mean.

The two step procedure attempts to identify those factors that significantly affect the signal-to-noise (SN) ratio and find the adjustment factors that markedly influence the mean.

> **EDITOR'S NOTE 1.25** A sentence is not parallel when using an infinitive **(to identify)** and a gerund **(finding)** are used together.

9. The adjustment factors are found by selection of the appropriate levels and to vary the surrounding factors.

The adjustment factors are found by selecting the appropriate levels and varying the surrounding factors.

EDITOR'S NOTE 1.26 A sentence is not parallel when a noun *(selection)* and an infinitive *(to vary)* are used together.

10. Being a volatile compound, the chemist handled the mixture with extreme caution.

Because the mixture was a volatile compound, the chemist handled it with extreme caution.

EDITOR'S NOTE 1.27 In this sentence, *the mixture* rather than *the chemist* was *a volatile compound*. The revised sentence eliminates the dangling modifier.

11. The new computer has many improved functions that reached the market last week.

The new computer that reached the market last week has many improved functions.

EDITOR'S NOTE 1.28 A common mistake of technical writers is the use of a misplaced modifier when the clause or phrase does not clearly modify what it should. In the revised sentence, the modifying clause *that reached the market last week* is placed next to what it should modify, *The new computer,* thus eliminating confusion.

12.   The modem offered by the manufacturer with the latest functions has

many advantages over older models.

**The modem with the latest functions offered by the manufacturer has many
advantages over older models.**

> *EDITOR'S NOTE 1.29* Placing the modifying phrase *with the latest functions* in the wrong place
> erroneously states that *the manufacturer* not *the modem* has the latest functions.

that of

13.   The input's power is greater than the output.

The input's power is greater than that of the output.

> *EDITOR'S NOTE 1.30* The comparison in this sentence is illogical. Instead of comparing *power* to *the
> input,* either *power* is compared to *power* or *input* is compared to *input*. The revised sentence makes the
> sentence logical.

to

14.   The back propagation network can be used estimate the mapping

function between the two variables.

**The back propagation network can be used to estimate the mapping function
between the two variables.**

> *EDITOR'S NOTE 1.31* Make sure that necessary words are not missing. Otherwise, the meaning will be
> unclear.

than conventional ones

15.   The novel algorithm is more efficient in terms of computational cost.

**The novel algorithm is more efficient than conventional ones in terms of com-
putational cost.**

16. Turn on the machine and the valve should be closed.

Turn on the machine and close the valve.

> *EDITOR'S NOTE 1.32* The writer should avoid shifting moods, particularly from imperative (i.e., stating a command) to indicative (i.e., stating a fact or question).

17. The academic advisor asked the graduate student if the paper was completed and is it ready to send to the journal for review?

The academic advisor asked the graduate student if the paper was completed and ready to send to the journal for review.

> *EDITOR'S NOTE 1.33* The writer should avoid shifting from indirect course (i.e., reporting what the speaker said) to direct course(i.e., stating the actual words of the speaker), or vice versa.

18. The laboratory manager arranged the meeting and the discussion was led by him.

The laboratory manager arranged the meeting and led the discussion.

> *EDITOR'S NOTE 1.34* Shifting the subject from *laboratory manager* to *discussion* makes this sentence less emphatic and confuses the reader from identifying the important subject.

Exercise 3

Correct the following sentences using the copyediting marks on page 1.

1. Everyone are planning to attend the event.

2. The simulation program that was designed to identify consumer tastes are ready for implementation.

3. *War and Peace* continue to be a widely read novel.

4. When alternative methods attempt to analyze unknown variables in an experiment, they have limitations.

5. The amount of computation on their method is less than the original MLE method, but it still requires much computational effort.

6. The proposed procedure can be easily implemented in an industrial setting. This is despite the fact that it lacks a rigorous theoretical justification.

7. The SN ratio allows optimization of the parameter design procedure and that this procedure is decomposed into two smaller optimization steps.

8. The proposed method is accurate, effective and does not cost that much.

9. The derived solution not only provides a feasible strategy, but also measurements of the position are accurate.

10. To host an international conference, many considerations must be made by the organizing committee.

11. After completing the assigned homework, the final examination was taken.

12. Identifying the unknown variables, the case study was deemed successful.

13. Their computer resembles the IBM system more than the Apple system.

Exercise 3

14. The university network is as quick, if not quicker than, the public one.

15. A president's authority is usually greater than a department chairman.

16.   After the researcher completes the experiment, you should put away

all laboratory equipment.

17. The variables can be easily calculated because it is relatively simple.

18. The statistical regression method was used to identify the relationship

between the geometric orientation and correction ratio; a set of

input/output patterns is also applied.

Answers

Exercise 3

1. Everyone ~~are~~ *is* planning to attend the event.

Everyone is planning to attend the event.

> *EDITOR'S NOTE 1.35* Although pronouns like **everyone** or **everybody** may imply more than one person, the writer should not mistakenly choose a plural verb. Singular verbs should be used for the following pronouns: *anybody, anyone, each, either, every, everybody, everyone, neither, nobody, no one, one, somebody, someone,* and *something.*

2. The simulation program that was designed to identify consumer tastes ~~are~~ *is* ready for implementation.

The simulation program that was designed to identify consumer tastes is ready for implementation.

> *EDITOR'S NOTE 1.36* Writers should be careful not to choose the wrong verb form by becoming distracted by words or phrases between the subject and the verb.

3. War and Peace continue*s* to be a widely read novel.

<u>War and Peace</u> continues to be a widely read novel.

> *EDITOR'S NOTE 1.37* Even if the subject is in plural form, names of companies or titles of books or plays should use a singular verb. Also, book titles should be underlined.

4.   When alternative methods attempt ~~ing~~ to analyze unknown variables in an

experiment, ~~they~~ have limitations.

When attempting to analyze unknown variables in an experiment, alternative methods have limitations.

OR

Alternative methods have limitations when attempting to analyze unknown variables in an experiment.

Although having less

5.   ~~The amount of~~ computation ~~on their method is less~~ than the original

their method

MLE method, ~~but it~~ still requires much computational effort.

Although having less computation than the original MLE method, their method still requires much implementation.

OR

Their method, although having less computation than the original MLE method, still requires much implementation.

6.   The proposed procedure can be easily implemented in an industrial

, although   _ing_

setting. ~~This is despite the fact that it lacks~~ a rigorous theoretical justification.

The proposed procedure, although lacking a rigorous theoretical justification, can be easily implemented in an industrial setting.

OR

Although lacking a rigorous theoretical justification, the proposed procedure can be easily implemented in an industrial setting.

7.   The SN ratio allows optimization of the parameter design procedure and ~~that this procedure~~ is decomposed into two smaller optimization steps.

The SN ratio allows the parameter design procedure to be optimized and decomposed into two smaller optimization steps.

> *EDITOR'S NOTE 1.38* A sentence is not parallel when a noun (optimization) and a clause (that this procedure is decomposed into two smaller optimization steps) are used together.

8.   The proposed method is accurate, effective and ~~does not cost that much~~. inexpensive.

The proposed method is accurate, effective, and inexpensive.

9.   The derived solution not only provides a feasible strategy, but also measurements of the position are accurate.

The derived solution not only provides a feasible strategy, but also accurately measures the position.

10.   To host an international conference, many considerations must be made by the organizing committee.

To host an international conference, the organizing committee must make many considerations.

OR

The organizing committee must make many considerations when hosting an international conference.

11.   After completing the assigned homework, the final examination was taken.

After the student completed the assigned homework, the final examination was taken.

OR

The student took the final examination after completing the assigned homework.

12.   Identifying the unknown variables, the case study was deemed successful.

After the students identified the unknown variables, the case study was deemed successful.

OR

The case study was deemed successful after the students identified the unknown variables.

13.   The computer resembles the IBM system more than *it resembles* the Apple system.

Their computer resembles the IBM system more than it resembles the Apple system.

14.   The university network is as quick *as*, if not quicker than, the public one.

The university network is as quick as, if not quicker than, the public one.

15.   A president's authority is usually greater than *that of* a department chairman.

A president's authority is usually greater than that of a department chairman.

OR

A president's authority is usually greater than a department chairman's.

16.   After the researcher completes the experiment, you should put away all laboratory equipment.

After completing the experiment, the researcher should put away all laboratory equipment.

OR

After the researcher completes the experiment, all of the laboratory equipment should be put away.

17.   The variables can be easily calculated because ~~it is~~ *they are* relatively simple.

The variables can be easily calculated because they are relatively simple.

OR

The variables can be easily calculated owing to their simplicity.

18.   The statistical regression method was used to identify the relationship between the geometric orientation and correction ratio; a set of input/output patterns ~~is~~ *was* also applied.

The statistical regression method was used to identify the relationship between the geometric orientation and correction ratio; a set of input/output patterns was also applied.

Unit Two
Ensure subject and verb agreement

單元二 ： 主詞及動詞必須前後呼應

The reader becomes confused when the verb does not agree with its subject. Subject and verb disagreement not only creates confusion over how many people, places or objects are involved, but also gives the sentence a faulty logic. A major reason for subject-verb disagreement is failing to recognize the subject and the verb. 如果主詞的單複數與動詞不能配合，不僅讀者感到困惑，同時句子的邏輯也會發生問題。

Consider the following examples:

Original
The number of participants in the study have increased.
Revised
The number of participants in the study has increased.

Original
Physics as well as Economics are difficult subjects in school.
Revised
Physics and Economics are difficult subjects in school.

Original
Either the company or stockholders is responsible for the financial loss.
Revised
Either the company or stockholders are responsible for the financial loss.

Original
My companion and friend are my wife.
Revised
My companion and friend is my wife.
OR
My wife is my companion and friend.

Exercise 4

Circle the correct form of the verb or pronoun in the following sentences. Make any other necessary corrections.

1. A number of innovative developments (has , have) been made in the multi-component injection molding process in recent years.

2. A gas channel design that (guides , guide) the gas flow to the desired locations (is , are) one of the key factors that determine a successful application.

3. The delay time along with gas injection points (is , are) important in producing injection-molded parts of quality.

4. Neither the processing parameters nor the amount of polymer melt injection solely (determine , determines) a successful gas channel design.

5. To select the number and locations of gas injection points and to determine the amount of polymer melt injection (is , are) essential to a successful application.

Exercise 4

6.   Ergonomics (aim , aims) to integrate worker comfort and productivity.

7.   Each of the factors (contribute , contributes) to a successful design.

8.   The simulation in which the polymer melt flow (occurs , occur) in thin cavities (provides , provide) accurate predictions.

9.   Establishing a general model or empirical formula in addition to describing the thickness variation of the skin melt that exists between the gas/melt interface and the cavity wall (appear , appears) to be necessary for further development.

10.   The number of gas injection points (are , is) important in producing quality injection-molded parts.

11.   The majority of factors heavily (influences , influence) product performance.

12.   Accurately determining the interface shape of a bubble nose and properly selecting the film thickness (is , are) of primary concern.

Answers
Exercise 4

1. A number of innovative developments (has , (have)) been made in the
    Multi-component injection molding process in recent years.

    > **EDITOR'S NOTE 2.1** ***The number of*** takes singular verb while ***A number of*** takes a plural verb.

2. A gas channel design that ((guides) , guide) the gas flow to
    the desired locations ((is) , are) one of the key factors that determine
    a successful application.

3. The delay time along with gas injection points ((is) , are) important in
    producing injection-molded parts of quality.

    OR

    The delay time along with gas injection points (is , are) important in produc-
    ing injection-molded parts of quality.

    > **EDITOR'S NOTE 2.2** As mentioned earlier, expressions such as ***as well as, in addition to, along with,***
    > ***accompanied by*** and ***with*** should not confuse the reader into thinking that the sentence has a com-
    > pound subject and, therefore, should have a plural verb. The verb in this sentence should be singular
    > since the subject, ***The delay time*** , is singular in form.

Exercise 4

4. Neither the processing parameters nor the amount of polymer melt injection solely (determine , determines) a successful gas channel design.

> ***EDITOR'S NOTE 2.3*** The verb in the sentence is singular in form since ***the amount of polymer injection***, not ***the processing parameters***, is the closest to the verb.

5. To select the number and locations of gas injection points and to determine the amount of polymer melt injection (is , are) essential to a successful application.

> ***EDITOR'S NOTE 2.4*** A compound subject, ***To select the number and locations of gas injection points*** and ***to determine the amount of polymer melt injection,*** takes a plural verb.

6. Ergonomics (aim , aims) to integrate worker comfort and productivity.

7. Each of the factors (contribute , contributes) to a successful design.

   OR

   Each factor contributes to a successful design.

8.　The simulation in which the polymer melt flow ((occurs), occur) in

thin cavities ((provides), provide) accurate predictions.

> **EDITOR'S NOTE 2.5** Writers should be careful not to choose the wrong verb form by becoming
> distracted by words or phrases between the subject and the verb.

9.　Establishing a general model or empirical formula in addition to

describing the thickness variation of the skin melt that exists between

the gas/melt interface and the cavity wall (appear , (appears)) to be

necessary for further development.

10.　The number of gas injection points (are , (is)) important in producing

quality injection-molded parts.

11.　The majority of factors heavily (influences , (influence)) product

performance.

> **EDITOR'S NOTE 2.6** The verb should be plural in this sentence since the noun refers to <u>individual</u>
> factors.

12.　Accurately determining the interface shape of a bubble nose and

properly selecting the film thickness (is , (are)) of primary concern.

Exercise 5

Circle the correct form of the verb or pronoun for the following sentences. Make any other necessary corrections.

1. Either gas delay time or mold temperatures (impacts , impact) the surface tension.

2. My advisor and friend (are , is) Professor Wu.

3. Economics (plays , play) a major role in many business decisions.

4. Everybody (try , tries) to create and market a product during the course.

5. One of the hidden nodes that (was , were) implemented in the neural network learning algorithms (was , were) extensively studied.

6. There (is , are) many topics to be covered during the seminar.

7.   Verification of the generalization capability of the neural model, along with identification of the best forecast of the performance measure, (demonstrates , demonstrate) the efficiency of the network in establishing the optimal parameter society.

8.   A number of parameter setup values in a gas-assisted injection molding process (are , is) identified.

9.   Evaluation of the effect of various parameters and identification of the optimal parameter setup values in a gas-assisted injection molding process (is , are) performed in this study.

10. The majority of the group (confers , confer) with the school's decision.

11. The majority of the parameter setups (was , were) constructed for network testing.

12. The design parameter as well as processing parameters (makes , make) the proposed approach more effective.

Answers

Exercise 5

1.   Either gas delay time or mold temperatures (impacts , (impact)) the

surface tension.

2.   My advisor and friend (are , (is)) Professor Wu.

OR

Professor Wu is my advisor and friend.

3.   Economics ((plays), play) a major role in many business decisions.

4.   Everybody (try , (tries)) to create and market a product during the

course.

5.   One of the hidden nodes that (was , (were)) implemented in the neural

network learning algorithms ((was), were) extensively studied.

6.   There (is , (are)) many topics to be covered during the seminar.

EDITOR'S NOTE 2.7 The noun following the verb determines whether the verb is singular or plural since *there is* or *there are* is not the subject. If you are still confused as to whether a sentence beginning with *There* takes a singular or plural form, place the subject in front of the sentence. Consider the following example:

Original
There (is , are) many computer courses available at the university.
Revised
Many computer courses are available at the university.

Placing the subject in front of the sentence makes it clear as to whether the verb should take a singular or plural form.

7. Verification of the generalization capability of the neural model, along with identification of the best forecast of the performance measure, (demonstrates, demonstrate) the efficiency of the network in establishing the optimal parameter society.

8. A number of parameter setup values in a gas-assisted injection molding process ((are), is) identified.

9. Evaluation of the effect of various parameters and identification of the optimal parameter setup values in a gas-assisted injection molding process (is , are) performed in this study.

10.   The majority of the group (confers , confer) with the school's decision.

> ***EDITOR'S NOTE 2.8*** Avoid wordiness by saying **Most** instead of **The majority of.**

11 . The majority of the parameter setups (was , were) constructed for

network testing.

12.   The design parameter as well as processing parameters (makes , make)

the proposed approach more effective.

Exercise 6

Circle the correct form of the verb or pronoun for the following sentences. Make any other necessary corrections.

1. Either the collected data set or two additional outputs (was , were) used

   to construct a neural network model.

2. The research assistant and the doctoral candidate (is , are) the same

   person.

3. Physics (make , makes) most first year doctoral students nervous.

4. The acoustics in the auditorium (are , is) excellent.

5. Everyone (is , are) planning to attend the convocation in order that the

   public becomes more aware of the issue.

6. The order of experimental steps (were , was) carefully arranged in order

   to avoid repetition.

7. There (is , are) a number of web search engines available in Taiwan.

8. Detailed information about the thickness variations that (exists , exist) between the gas/melt interface and the cavity wall can be found elsewhere.

9. What kind of limitations (does , do) the process engineer face in a simulated environment?

10. More than one position (was , were) taken on the environmental issue for the reason that diverse opinions could be shared.

11. To exert uniform pressure on the molded part until it is sufficiently solidified and injected and to substantially reduce operating expenses in terms of material costs (is , are) relevant tasks during the post-filling stage.

12. The majority of the faculty (feels , feel) that constructing a new facility would encourage new students to enroll in the program.

Answers

Exercise 6

1. Either the collected data set or two additional outputs (was , (were)) used to construct a neural network model.

2. The research assistant and the doctoral candidate ((is) , are) the same person.

3. Physics (make , (makes)) most first year doctoral students nervous.

4. The acoustics in the auditorium ((are) , is) excellent.

5. Everyone ((is) , are) planning to attend the convocation in order that the public becomes more aware of the issue.

> **EDITOR'S NOTE 2.9** Avoid wordiness by saying **so** instead of **in order that.**

6. The order of experimental steps (were , (was)) carefully arranged in order to avoid repetition.

> **EDITOR'S NOTE 2.10** Avoid redundancy by saying **to** or **for** instead of **in order to.**

Exercise 6

7.   There (is , are) a number of web search engines available in Taiwan.

8.   Detailed information about the thickness variations that (exists , exist) between the gas/melt interface and the cavity wall can be found elsewhere.

9.   What kind of limitations (does , do) the process engineer face in a simulated environment?

10.   More than one position (was , were) taken on the environmental issue for the reason that diverse opinions could be shared.

> **EDITOR'S NOTE 2.11** Avoid wordiness by saying *so* instead of **for the reason that.**

11.   To exert uniform pressure on the molded part until it is sufficiently solidified and injected and to substantially reduce operating expenses in terms of material costs (is , are) relevant tasks during the post-filling stage.

12.   The majority of the faculty (feels , feel) that constructing a new facility would encourage new students to enroll in the program.

Exercise 7

Circle the correct form of the verb or pronoun for the following sentences. Make any other necessary corrections.

1.   Genetics (has , have) drawn increasing interest in recent years.

2.   A statistical Taguchi approach in addition to a backpropagation neural network model (is, are) developed in this study.

3.   Neither conventional models nor previous literature (address , addresses) the backpropagation delay problem in this structure.

4.   Unknown variables or time significantly (influence , influences) the product quality when the machine parts are in close proximity to each other.

5.   The number of theoretical investigations on bubble/liquid displacement in a tube (is , are) increasing.

6.   The physical phenomena associated with gas penetration within the polymer melt (require , requires) further clarification.

Exercise 7

7. Neither of the conditions markedly (affects , affect) gas penetration within the polymer melt much.

8. Members of the scientific community that (studies , study) genetic similarities between rats and humans (is , are) divided on the issue.

9. Either surface tensions or thickness ratio (plays , play) an important role in determining the interface shape of a bubble nose.

10. Each of the conditions (is , are) far more complicated than reported in the above studies.

11. Melt temperature accompanied by mold temperature in all cases (impact , impacts) skin melt thickness.

12. To test the constructed network model and to identify the real optimal parameter setup (is , are) of primary concern in this study.

Answers
Exercise 7

1. Genetics ((has), have) drawn increasing interest in recent years.

2. A statistical Taguchi approach in addition to a backpropagation neural network model ((is), are) developed in this study.

3. Neither conventional models nor previous literature (address , (addresses)) the backpropagation delay problem in this structure.

4. Unknown variables or time significantly (influence , (influences)) the product quality when the machine parts are in close proximity to each other.

    EDITOR'S NOTE 2.12 Avoid wordiness by saying **near** instead of **in close proximity to.**

5. The number of theoretical investigations on bubble/liquid displacement in a tube ((is), are) increasing.

Exercise 7

6.   The physical phenomena associated with gas penetration within the polymer melt (require , requires) further clarification.

7.   Neither of the conditions (affects , affect) gas penetration within the polymer melt much.

> **EDITOR'S NOTE 2.13** Depending on the sentence's context, *significantly*, *markedly*, and *substantially* can be used as alternatives to *much* and *greatly* when the Chinese meaning is 很多.

8.   Members of the scientific community that (studies , study) genetic similarities between rats and humans (is , are) divided on the issue.

9.   Either surface tensions or thickness ratio (plays , play) an important role in determining the interface shape of a bubble nose.

> **EDITOR'S NOTE 2.14** Depending on the sentence's context, *critical, crucial, essential, pertinent, relevant, significant* and *vital* can be used as alternatives to *important* when the Chinese meaning is 重要.

10.   Each of the conditions (is , are) far more complicated than reported in the above studies.

11.　Melt temperature accompanied by mold temperature in all cases (impact

, impacts) skin melt thickness.

> **EDITOR'S NOTE 2.15** *Avoid wordiness by saying* always *instead of* in all cases.

12.　To test the constructed network model and to identify the real optimal

parameter setup (is , are) of primary concern in this study.

Ensure that pronoun references are clear in meaning

單元三 ： 代名詞必須清楚的使用

Readers become confused when the sentences they are reading contain pronouns that do not have a clear antecedent. An antecedent is what a pronoun is referring to. Many problems can arise when a pronoun does not refer to a clear antecedent. For instance, a pronoun can refer to more than one antecedent.
如果代名詞所指的人物或事物不能交待清楚，也是徒增讀者困惑。

For instance, a pronoun can refer to more than one antecedent. Consider the following example:

The instructor informed the student that she must leave the classroom early.

In the sentence, confusion over who **she** refers to, the **instructor** or the **student**, makes the reader wonder who must leave the classroom early. If **she** refers to the **student**, then the sentence's intended meaning can be expressed as

The instructor informed the student, "You must leave the classroom early."
OR
The instructor informed the student to leave the classroom early.

Another problem is that placing the pronoun far away from its antecedent makes it more difficult for the reader to understand what the pronoun refers to. Consider the following example:

The chemist slowly poured the mixture into the flask and waited until the temperature reached boiling temperature; it lasted for five minutes.

In the sentence, the reader will have difficulty in understand what the antecedent refers to since it is far away from its antecedent. Clearly stating what **it** refers to omits confusion and, therefore, the revised sentence should read as follows:

The chemist slowly poured the mixture into the flask and waited until the temperature reached boiling temperature; the procedure lasted for five minutes.

Yet another area of confusion caused by improper use of antecedents involves using **which**, **this**, and **that** when referring to a previous clause of sentence. Consider thefollowing:

The procedure lasts several minutes, which complicates the overall manufacturing process.

In the sentence, **which** may create confusion over what the writer is referring to. The following revisions can omit this potential confusion:

The procedure lasts several minutes, thereby complicating the overall manufacturing process.
OR
The procedure lasting several minutes complicates the overall manufacturing process.
OR
The fact that the procedure lasts several minutes complicates the overall manufacturing process.
OR
The procedure lasts several minutes; this time period complicates the overall manufacturing process.

Other examples of improper antecedent use are found in the following exercises.

Exercise 8

Correct the following sentences using the copyediting marks on page 1.

1. The machines can process the family of parts, ensuring that it reaches full capacity.

2. All parts have the same transportation costs, which limits the effectiveness of traditional approaches.

3. The team attempts to optimize the thickness by minimizing the variation and maintaining the desired mean. This accounts for why the effects of process parameters on the silicon nitride deposition process are studied.

4. In previous literature, they do not examine the feasibility of incorporating PS into SA to develop a more efficient stochastic optimization approach at such time as the variables are constant.

5. The department chairman told the research assistant that she needed to perform the simulations in the event that the experiment fails.

6. Deterioration is set to a constant fraction of the stock level, which implies that shortages are not permitted and the demand rate is assumed to decrease exponentially.

7. When a machine is assigned to a manufacturing cell, it attempts to reduce the total cost.

8. The posterior objective concentrates on balancing intracell and intercell machine loadings, which allows us to formulate the cell formation problem as follows.

9. Factors C, D, F, G and H significantly affect the response average. This indicates that F can be adjusted based on the target value.

10. You should maintain a constant cutting speed even though the effective diameter of the cutting changes during machining.

Exercise 8

11. In most previous investigations, they do not consider the simultaneous effects of deterioration and inflation.

12. A numerical example demonstrates the effectiveness of the proposed method, which further indicates that the total system cost will be incorrectly estimated if the deteriorating effect and/or inflationary effect are neglected.

Answers

Exercise 8

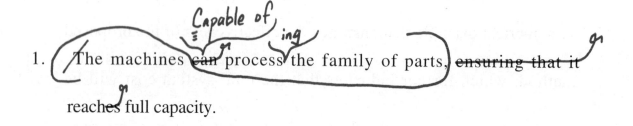

1. The machines can process the family of parts, ensuring that it reaches full capacity.

Capable of processing the family of parts, the machines reach full capacity.

OR

The machines, capable of processing the family of parts, reach full capacity.

2. All parts have the same transportation costs, which limits the effectiveness of traditional approaches.

All parts have the same transportation costs, thus limiting the effectiveness of traditional approaches.

OR

The fact that all parts have the same transportation costs limits the effectiveness of traditional approaches.

OR

All parts having the same transportation costs limit the effectiveness of traditional approaches.

OR

All parts have the same transportation costs; this situation limits the effectiveness of traditional approaches.

OR

The effectiveness of traditional approaches is limited since all parts have the same transportation costs.

> *EDITOR'S NOTE 3.1* As mentioned earlier, using *which* to refer to a previous clause may make it difficult for the reader to understand what is being referred to. The above revised sentences avoid confusion over whether *which* refers to *all parts, the same transportation costs* or *all parts having the same transportation costs.*

> *EDITOR'S NOTE 3.2* Depending on the sentence's context, *conventional, available* or *existing* can be used as alternatives to *traditional* when the Chinese meaning is 傳統.

3.   The team attempts to optimize the thickness by minimizing the

attempt

variation and maintaining the desired mean. This accounts for why

the effects of process parameters on the silicon nitride deposition

process are studied.

The team attempts to optimize the thickness by minimizing the variation and maintaining the desired mean. This attempt accounts for why the effects of process parameters on the silicon nitride deposition process are studied.

> *EDITOR'S NOTE 3.3* As mentioned earlier, beginning a sentence with *This* or *That* to refer to a previous sentence may make it difficult for the reader to understand what is being referred to. Simply turning the verb of the previous sentence into the subject of the following can clarify the writer's intended meaning, as done in this revised sentence.

4. ~~In~~ previous literature, ~~they do~~ not examine the feasibility of incorporating PS into SA to develop a more efficient stochastic optimization approach at such times as the two variables are constant.

Previous literature does not examine the feasibility of incorporating PS into SA to develop a more efficient stochastic optimization approach.

EDITOR'S NOTE 3.4 Avoid wordiness by saying *when* instead of *at such times as.*

5. The department chairman told the research assistant ~~that she~~ needed to perform the simulations in the event that the experiment fails.

The department chairman told the research assistant, "You need to perform the simulations in the event that the experiment fails."

EDITOR'S NOTE 3.5 Avoid wordiness by saying *if* instead of **in the event that.**

The fact that,

6. Deterioration is set to a constant fraction of the stock level, ~~which~~ implies that shortages are not permitted and the demand rate is assumed to decrease exponentially.

The fact that deterioration is set to a constant fraction of the stock level implies that shortages are not permitted and the demand rate is assumed to decrease exponentially.

OR

Deterioration is set to a constant fraction of the stock level, implying that shortages are not permitted and the demand rate is assumed to decrease exponentially.

OR

Setting deterioration to a constant fraction of the stock level implies that shortages are not permitted and the demand rate is assumed to decrease exponentially.

OR

Deterioration is set to a constant fraction of the stock level; this situation implies that shortages are not permitted and the demand rate is assumed to decrease exponentially.

7.   When a machine is assigned to a manufacturing cell, it attempts to reduce the total cost.

When assigned to a manufacturing cell, a machine attempts to reduce the total cost.

OR

A machine attempts to reduce the total cost when assigned to a manufacturing cell.

OR

A machine, when assigned to a manufacturing cell, attempts to reduce the total cost.

OR

Reducing the total cost is the desired goal when a machine is assigned to a manufacturing cell.

The fact that

8. The posterior objective concentrates on balancing intracell and intercell machine loadings, which allows us to formulate the cell formation problem as follows.

The fact that the posterior objective concentrates on balancing intracell and intercell machine loadings allows us to formulate the cell formation problem as follows.

OR

The posterior objective concentrates on balancing intracell and intercell machine loadings, allowing us to formulate the cell formation problem as follows.

OR

The posterior objective concentrates on balancing intracell and intercell machine loadings; this balance allows us to formulate the cell formation problem as follows.

9. Factors C, D, F, G and H significantly affect the response average.
finding (observation, occurrence phenomenon, events)
This indicates that F can be adjusted based on the target value.

Factors C, D, F, G and H significantly affect the response average. This finding (observation, occurrence, phenomenon, event) indicates that F can be adjusted based on the target value.

10. You should maintain a constant cutting speed even though the effective diameter of the cutting changes during machining.

A constant cutting speed should be maintained even though the effective diameter of the cutting changes during machining.

OR

Maintaining a constant speed is desired even though the effective diameter of the cutting changes during machining.

11. In most previous investigations, they do not consider the simultaneous effects of deterioration and inflation.

Most previous investigations do not consider the simultaneous effects of deterioration and inflation.

12. A numerical example demonstrates the effectiveness of the proposed method, which further indicates that the total system cost will be incorrectly estimated if the deteriorating effect and/or inflationary effect are neglected.

A numerical example demonstrating the effectiveness of the proposed method further indicates that the total system cost will be incorrectly estimated if the deteriorating effect and/or inflationary effect are neglected.

OR

A numerical example demonstrates the effectiveness of the proposed method, further indicating that the total system cost will be incorrectly estimated if the deteriorating effect and/or inflationary effect are neglected.

Exercise 9

Correct the following sentences using the copyediting marks on page 1.

1. Cell formation is the first and most difficult step in CMS design in that it identifies parts with similar processing requirements and the set of machines capable of processing the corresponding family of parts.

2. Taguchi's two-step procedure is in many cases inefficient if certain conditions are not satisfied, which may prevent this procedure from attaining the minimum quality loss despite a maximized SN ratio.

3. Factors A, C, E, F and H significantly affect SN. This means that a larger SN ratio has a better quality.

4. It is widely recognized that a constant speed can be obtained if the spindle speed does not vary.

5. Their consumption rate item in most cases stipulates that its demand rate depends on the stock level when it is increasing.

6.   As the machine operator, you must assume that a hazardous situation could occur on the shop floor at any time.

7.   Developing a more feasible approach to resolve the MCG problem is very difficult when it contains many unknown variables.

8.   The regression coefficient is statistically significant, which implies that a significant relationship exists in the following form.

9.   Only the first-order interaction effect is considered. This is since the second-order or higher-order interaction effect can generally be ignored in industry.

10. You know that the Internet has significantly affected commercial activity worldwide.

11. It is the responsibility of the department chairman to handle all administrative matters.

12. On the shop floor, it is a standard safety precaution for workers to wear a safety helmet.

Answers
Exercise 9

1. Cell formation is the first and most difficult step in CMS design in that it identifies parts with similar processing requirements and the set of machines capable of processing the corresponding family of parts.

    Cell formation, the first and most difficult step in CMS design, identifies parts with similar processing requirements and the set of machines capable of processing the corresponding family of parts.

    OR

    As the first and most difficult step in CMS design, cell formation identifies parts with similar processing requirements and the set of machines capable of processing the corresponding family of parts.

2. Taguchi's two-step procedure is in many cases inefficient if certain conditions are not satisfied, which may prevent this procedure from attaining the minimum quality loss despite a maximized SN ratio.

    Taguchi's two-step procedure is often inefficient if certain conditions are not satisfied, possibly preventing it from attaining the minimum quality loss despite a maximized SN ratio.

    > **EDITOR'S NOTE 3.6** To avoid repeating *procedure* twice in the same sentence, the revision replaces the second *procedure it* because it has a clear referent.

    > **EDITOR'S NOTE 3.7** Avoid wordiness by saying *always* instead of *in many cases*.

finding (observation, occurrence)

3. Factors A, C, E, F and H significantly affect SN. This means that a

    larger SN ratio has a better quality.

    Factors A, C, E, F and H significantly affect SN. This finding (observation, occurrence, phenomenon, event) means that a larger SN ratio has a better quality.

    > *EDITOR'S NOTE 3.8* Depending on the sentence's context, *implies* or *suggests* can be used as alternatives to *means* when the Chinese meaning is 意指.

As

4. ~~It is~~ widely recognized that a constant speed can be obtained if the

    spindle speed does not vary.

    As widely recognized, a constant speed can be obtained if the spindle speed does not vary.

5. Their consumption rate item in most cases stipulates that its demand

    rate depends on the stock level when it is increasing.

    Their consumption rate in most cases stipulates that its demand rate depends on an increasing stock level.

    > *EDITOR'S NOTE 3.9* In the sentence, what *is increasing* is unclear: *demand rate* or *stock level*. although the author's intended meaning is the latter.

    > *EDITOR'S NOTE 3.10* Avoid wordiness by saying *usually* instead of *in most cases*. Depending on the sentence's context, *generally, normally* or *typically* can be used as alternatives to *usually* when the Chinese meaning is 通常.

6. As the machine operator, you must assume that a hazardous situation could occur on the shop floor at any time.

The machine operator must assume that a hazardous situation could occur on the shop floor at any time.

7. Developing a more feasible approach to resolve the MCG problem is extremely difficult when it contains many unknown variables.

Developing a more feasible approach to resolve the MCG problem that contains many unknown variables is extremely difficult.

> ***EDITOR'S NOTE 3.11*** Depending on the sentence's context, ***extremely, rather, quite,*** or ***highly*** can be used as alternatives to ***very*** when the Chinese meaning is 非常.

8. The regression coefficient is statistically significant, which implies that a significant relationship exists in the following form.

Statistical significance of the regression coefficient implies that a significant relationship exists in the following form.

OR

The regression coefficient is statistically significant, implying that a significant relationship exists in the following form.

OR

The fact that the regression coefficient is statistically significant implies that a significant relationship exists in the following form

9. Only the first-order interaction effect is considered. ~~This is~~ since the

second-order or higher-order interaction effect can generally be

ignored in industry.

Only the first-order interaction effect is considered since the second-order or higher-order interaction effect can generally be ignored in industry.

10. ~~You know that~~ the Internet has significantly affected commercial

activity worldwide.

The Internet has significantly affected commercial activity worldwide.

11. ~~It is the~~ responsibility ~~of~~ the department chairman ~~to~~ handle all

administrative matters.

The department chairman is responsible for handling all administrative matters.

12. On the shop floor, it is a standard safety precaution for workers to

wear a safety helmet.

Wearing a safety helmet on the shop floor is a standard safety precaution for workers.

Exercise 10

Correct the following sentences using the copyediting marks on page 1.

1.   While the GA method searches along the contour of the optimized function, it makes no assumption about the problem space.

2.   The proposed technique is similar to industrial control charts, which makes it easily understood by the practitioner.

3.   Conventional approaches for analyzing censored data are computationally complicated and often difficult to explain to practitioners. That explains why this work presents an effective procedure based on the rank transformation of the responses.

4.   In Taiwan's semiconductor industry, they are applying state-of-the-art technologies in view of the fact that the island has a highly skilled labor force.

5.   Increasing parameter k increases the optimal ordering quantity. This

affects the total system cost as well.

6.   The optimal ordering quantity increases, which increases the total

system cost.

7.   The conveyor belt transports the machine part to the assembly line,

where it proceeds to the workstation.

8.   Taguchi's two-step procedure can identify optimal settings of the

design factors, which minimizes the expected quadratic loss when the

following conditions are met.

9.   In addition to the proposed procedure considering the variability of

the control factors,it can concurrently perform censored data analysis

for replicated and unreplicated experiments.

10. They showed in an earlier investigation [4] that the turned parts on CNC lathes have continuous forms.

11. They stated in their report the manner in which changes should be made.

12. The graduate student reported to the academic advisor that his experiments were almost finished.

Answers
Exercise 10

1. While the GA method searches along the contour of the optimized function, it makes no assumption about the problem space.

    While searching along the contour of the optimized function, the GA method does not make an assumption about the problem space.

2. The proposed technique is similar to industrial control charts, which makes it easily understood by the practitioner.

    The proposed technique's similarity to industrial control charts makes it easily understood by the practitioner.

    OR

    The proposed technique is similar to industrial control charts, making it easily understood by the practitioner.

    OR

    The fact that the proposed technique is similar to industrial control charts makes it easily understood by the practitioner.

    > ***EDITOR'S NOTE 3.12*** Depending on the sentence's intended meaning, ***resembles*** can be used as an alternative to ***is similar*** to when the Chinese meaning is 類似.

3. Conventional approaches for analyzing censored data are computationally complicated and often difficult to explain to practitioners. ~~That explains why~~ Therefore, this work presents an effective procedure based on the rank transformation of the responses.

    Conventional approaches for analyzing censored data are computationally complicated and often difficult to explain to practitioners. Therefore, this work presents an effective procedure based on the rank transformation of the responses.

4. Engineers

    In Taiwan's semiconductor industry, ~~they~~ are applying state-of-the-art technologies in view of the fact that the island has a highly skilled labor force.

    Engineers in Taiwan's semiconductor industry are applying state-of-the-art technologies in view of the fact that the island has a highly skilled labor force.

    > ***EDITOR'S NOTE 3.13*** Avoid wordiness by saying *because* or *since* as alternatives to *in view of the fact that*.

5. Increasing parameter k increases the optimal ordering quantity. This increase affects the total system cost as well.

    Increasing parameter k increases the optimal ordering quantity. This increase affects the total system cost as well.

    OR

In addition to increasing the optimal order quantity, increasing parameter k affects the total system cost as well.

> **EDITOR'S NOTE 3.14** Depending on the sentence's intended meaning, *impacts* or *influences* can be used as alternatives to **affects** when the Chinese meaning is 影響.

6.   The optimal ordering quantity increases, ~~which~~ increases the total system cost.

thereby / increasing

The optimal ordering quantity increases, thereby increasing the total system cost.

OR

Increasing the optimal ordering quantity increases the total system cost.

7.   The conveyor belt transports the machine part to the assembly line, ~~where it~~ proceeds to the workstation.

After transporting

After transporting the machine part to the assembly line, the conveyor belt proceeds to the workstation.

8.   Taguchi's two-step procedure can identify optimal settings of the design factors, ~~which~~ minimizes the expected quadratic loss when the following conditions are met.

thereby / minimizing

Taguchi's two-step procedure can identify optimal settings of the design factors, thereby minimizing the expected quadratic loss when the following conditions are met.

> *EDITOR'S NOTE 3.15* Depending on the sentence's context, **satisfy**, **fulfill** or **adhere** to can be used as alternatives to *meet* when the Chinese meaning is 滿足.

9. In addition to the proposed procedure considering the variability of the control factors, it can concurrently perform censored data analysis for replicated and unreplicated experiments.

    In addition to considering the variability of the control factors, the proposed procedure can concurrently perform censored data analysis for replicated and unreplicated experiments.

10. They showed in an earlier investigation [4] that the turned parts on CNC lathes have continuous forms.

    An earlier investigation [4] showed that the turned parts on CNC lathes have continuous forms.

> *EDITOR'S NOTE 3.16* Depending on the sentence's context, *demonstrate, verify, confirm, indicate,* or *reveal* can be used as alternatives to *show* when the Chinese meaning is 指出.

11. They stated in their report the manner in which changes should be made.

    Their report stated the manner in which changes should be made.

> *EDITOR'S NOTE 3.17* Avoid wordiness by saying *how* instead of *the manner in which*.

12. The graduate student reported to the academic advisor ~~that his~~

"My experiments ~~were~~ *are* almost finished."

The graduate student reported to the academic advisor, "My experiments are almost finished."

> *EDITOR'S NOTE 3.18* The revised sentence specifies whose experiments are almost finished, the graduate student's *not* the academic advisor's.

Exercise 11

Correct the following sentences using the copyediting marks on page 1.

1. It is our opinion that, when a decision reaches the final stage, it must be implemented promptly.

2. No adjustment factors exist if (C1) is violated, which means that the transformation approach can be carried out.

3. Taguchi [4] treated censoring times as actual failures, which may lead to serious deficiencies. This arises because the unobserved failure and censoring times may significantly differ.

4. A number of studies have examined how inflation affects an inventory policy, which also considered the time value of money and different inflation rates.

5. Increasing parameter k increases the optimal ordering quantity. This affects the total optimal total system cost.

6.   An optimal inventory policy which considers the simultaneous effects

of deterioration and inflation should be developed.

7.   Optimizing a large-scale problem to demonstrate the effectiveness of

the proposed approach is problematic when it adopts the integer

programming model.

8.   The uniformity of the output was unstable, which made it impossible

for engineers to adjust the process parameters when the wafer quality

did not match the required specifications.

9.   Besides their method relying on the existence of MLEs, it does not

consider the variability of control factors.

10.   Inventory replenishment policies are considered for deteriorating

items in a declining market under a continuous price increase. They

lead to a differential equation that describes the system's inventory

dynamics.

11. Driving a car and talking on a cellular phone at the same time is dangerous; this could cause an accident.

12. When different approaches employ variables to implement the procedure, they encounter several obstacles.

Answers

Exercise 11

1. It is our opinion that, when a decision reaches the final stage, it must

    be implemented promptly.

    It is opinion that, when reaching the final stage, a decision must be implemented promptly.

    OR

    It is our opinion that a decision must be implemented promptly when reaching the final stage.

    > **EDITOR'S NOTE 3.19** Avoid wordiness by saying *We believe* instead of *It is our opinion that.*

2. No adjustment factors exist if (C1) is violated, which means that the

    transformation approach can be carried out.

    The fact that no adjustment factors exist if (C1) is violated implies that the transformation approach can be carried out.

    OR

    No adjustment factors exist if (C1) is violated, implying that the transformation approach can be carried out.

    OR

    No adjustment factors exist if (C1) is violated; this violation implies that the transformation can be carried out.

    Or even better

The transformation approach can be carried out since no adjustment factors exist if (C1) is violated.

3. Taguchi [4] treated censoring times as actual failures, which may lead to serious deficiencies. This arises because the unobserved

    failure and censoring times may significantly differ.

    Taguchi [4] treated censoring times as actual failures, possibly leading to serious deficiencies. This situation (circumstance, phenomenon) arises because the unobserved failure and censoring times may significantly differ.

4. A number of studies have examined how inflation affects an inventory

    policy, which also considered the time value of money and different

    inflation rates.

    While examining how inflation affects an inventory policy, a number of studies also considered the time value of money and different inflation rates.

    OR

    In addition to examining how inflation affects an inventory policy, a number of studies also considered the time value of money and different inflation rates.

Exercise 11

EDITOR'S NOTE 3.22 Depending on the sentence's context, *several* or *many* can be used as alternatives to *a number of* when the Chinese meaning is 多幾個 or 很多.

5.   Increasing parameter k increases the optimal ordering quantity. This affects the total optimal total system cost.

Increasing parameter k increases the optimal ordering quantity, thus affecting the total optimal total system cost.

OR

Increasing parameter k increases the optimal ordering quantity. Such an increase affects the total optimal total system cost.

6.   An optimal inventory policy which considers the simultaneous effects of deterioration and inflation should be developed.

An optimal inventory policy capable of considering the simultaneous effects of deterioration and inflation should be developed.

7.   Optimizing a large-scale problem to demonstrate the effectiveness of the proposed approach is problematic when it adopts the integer programming model.

Optimizing a large-scale problem to demonstrate the effectiveness of the proposed approach is problematic when the latter adopts the integer programming model.

8. The uniformity of the output was unstable, ~~which made~~ *making* it impossible

    for engineers to adjust the process parameters when the wafer quality

    did not match the required specifications.

    **The uniformity of the output was unstable, making it impossible for engineers
    to adjust the process parameters when the wafer quality did not match the
    required specifications.**

    OR

    **The unstable uniformity of the output made it impossible for engineers to
    adjust the process parameters when the wafer quality did not match the
    required specifications.**

    OR

    **The fact that the uniformity of the output was unstable made it impossible for
    engineers to adjust the process parameters when the wafer quality did not
    match the required specifications.**

9. Besides their method relying on the existence of MLEs, it does not

    consider the variability of control factors.

    **Besides relying on the existence of MLEs, their method does not consider the
    variability of control factors.**

10. Inventory replenishment policies are considered for deteriorating

    items in a declining market under a continuous price increase. ~~They~~ *These policies*

    lead to a differential equation that describes the system's inventory

    dynamics.

Inventory replenishment policies are considered for deteriorating items in a declining market under a continuous price increase. These policies lead to a differential equation that describes the system's inventory dynamics.

11. Driving a car and talking on a cellular phone at the same time is

     habit

     dangerous; this could cause an accident.

Driving a car and talking on a cellular phone at the same time is dangerous; this habit could cause an accident.

> ***EDITOR'S NOTE 3.23*** Depending on the sentence's context, ***simultaneously*** or ***meanwhile*** can be used as alternatives to ***at the same time*** when the Chinese meaning is 同時.

12. When different approaches employ *ing* variables to implement the

     procedure, they encounter several obstacles.

When employing variables to implement the procedure, different approaches encounter several obstacles.

Or even better

Different approaches encounter several obstacles when employing variables to implement the procedure.

> ***EDITOR'S NOTE 3.24*** Depending on the sentence's context, ***various, varying, varied*** or ***distinct*** can be used as alternatives to ***different*** when the Chinese meaning is 不同.

Unit Four
Make sentences parallel in structure and meaning

單元四 ： 句子的結構須有一致性

Parallelism in technical writing means that all parts of a sentence must have a similar construction .
科技英文寫作中，句子的建構必須有一致性。

Consider the following example of a sentence that is not parallel:

The temperature rose to boiling point and the height was controlled by fluctuation of the variables.

In this sentence, putting the first part in active voice and the second part in passive voice creates an unbalanced feeling. The revision should read as

The temperature rose to boiling point and fluctuation of the variables controlled the height.

Consider another example of a sentence that is not parallel in structure:

Department managers must either assume sole responsibility for the success of a project or authority must be delegated to subordinates.

In this sentence, the correlative expression of **either…or** does not have a parallel structure. The revised sentence should read as

Department managers must either assume sole responsibility for the success of a project or delegate authority to subordinates. The committee should decide what to do immediately.

Yet another example of this parallel problem is

Success in school depends on the following:

Preparing for class assignments,
Consulting the teacher during office hours,
All textbook materials must be thoroughly read,
Getting at least seven hours of sleep daily, and
All appointments must be kept.

Sentences containing lists must be parallel in structure. The revised sentence should read as follows:

Success in school depends on the following:

Preparing for class assignments,
Consulting the teacher during office hours,
Thoroughly reading all textbook materials,
Getting at least seven hours of sleep daily, and
Keeping all appointments.

Other examples of sentences that are not parallel in structure and meaning are included in the following exercises.

Exercise 12

Correct the following sentences using the copyediting marks on page 1.

1. It is a fact that engineers select an appropriate variable and the transformed observations are treated as though they are normally distributed with a constant variance.

2. Those methods neither require previous knowledge of how the variables are distributed nor are the censored data stipulated to be available.

3. The procedure for analyzing singly censored data in a replicated experiment is as follows:

    Step 1: Distinguish the experimental results as the uncensored (complete) data and the censored (incomplete) data.

    Step 2: The relationship between the two values must be found by performing regression analysis.

Step 3: Estimate the two variables.

Step 4: The estimated censored data must be ranked.

Step 5: Find the regression models for response average and standard deviation for each trial.

Step 6: The factors that significantly affect the response average and standard deviation must be identified.

Step 7: The optimal factor/level combination must be determined.

4.   The derived model provides an extension of an earlier concept [1] and helping industrial managers in determining a feasible number of replenishments.

5.   Experimental design is used in this method to arrange the design   parameters and noise factors in the orthogonal arrays and computing the signal-to-noise (SN) ratio based on the quality loss for each experimental combination.

6. The relative importance of each response can be transformed into a fuzzy number through means of the establishment of a formal scale system that can be used to convert linguistic terms into their corresponding fuzzy numbers and to express the relative importance of each response by the linguistic term.

7. The Taguchi approach provides a combination of experimental design techniques with quality loss considerations and that the average quadratic loss is minimized.

8. The conventional approach happens to be cumbersome, complicated and wastes too much time.

9. The two-step procedure not only identifies those factors that significantly affect the signal-to-noise (SN) ratio, but also the levels that maximize SN are found.

10. Logethetis (1988) proved that strong non-linearities exist and the *B* technique was also recommended for use by him.

11. This work not only proposes an effective procedure based on the rank transformation of responses and regression analysis, but also the singly censored data are discussed.

12. The following steps describe the procedure:

Step 1: Calculate the normalized decision matrix.

Step 2: The weighted normalized decision matrix is calculated.

Step 3: The ideal and negative-ideal solution is determined.

Step 4: Calculate the separation measures.

Step 5: The relative closeness to the ideal solution is calculated.

Step 6: The preference order is ranked.

Answers
Exercise 12

1. It is a fact that engineers select an appropriate variable and the

    transformed observations are treated as though they are normally

    distributed with a constant variance.

    It is a fact that engineers select an appropriate variable and treat the trans-
    formed observations as though they are normally distributed with a constant
    variance.

    EDITOR'S NOTE 4.1 Omit *It is a fact that* since it does not add to the sentence's meaning. Other
    examples of needless phrases include *It is well known that, It goes without saying that, It may be said*
    that, It is evident that, It has been found that, and *It has long been known that.*

2. Those methods neither require previous knowledge of how the

    variables are distributed nor are the censored data stipulated to be

    available.

    Those methods neither require previous knowledge of how the variables are
    distributed nor stipulate availability of the censored data.

3. The procedure for analyzing singly censored data in a replicated

    experiment is as follows:

Step 1: Distinguish the experimental results as the uncensored (complete) data and the censored (incomplete) data.

Step 2: ~~Find~~ The relationship between the two values ~~must be found~~ by performing regression analysis.

Step 3: Estimate the two variables.

Step 4: The estimated censored data ~~must be~~ ranked.

Step 5: Find the regression models for response avaerage and standard deviation for each trial.

Step 6: The factors that significantly affect the response average and standard deviation ~~must be~~ identified.

Step 7: The optimal factor/level combination ~~must be~~ determined.

The procedure for analyzing singly censored data in a replicated experiment is as follows:

Step 1: Distinguish the experimental results as the uncensored (complete) data and the censored (incomplete) data.

Step 2: Find the relationship between the two values by performing regression analysis.

Step 3: Estimate the two variables.

Step 4: Rank the estimated censored data.

Step 5: Find the regression models for response average and standard deviation for each trial.

Step 6: Identify the factors that significantly affect the response average and standard deviation.

Step 7: Determine the optimal factor/level combination.

EDITOR'S NOTE 4.2 Depending on the sentence's context, *obtain, derive, attain, identify* or *distinguish* can be used as alternatives to *find* when the Chinese meaning is 找.

4.   The derived model ~~provides an extension of~~ an earlier concept [1] and helping industrial managers in determining a feasible number of replenishments.

The derived model extends an earlier concept [1] and helps industrial managers in determining a feasible number of replenishments.

EDITOR'S NOTE 4.3 Depending on the sentence's context, *assist, facilitate, guide, and direct* can be used as alternatives to *help* when the Chinese meaning is 幫助.

5. Experimental design is used in this method to arrange the design parameters and noise factors in the orthogonal arrays and computing the signal-to-noise (SN) ratio based on the quality loss for each experimental combination.

Experimental design is used in this method to arrange the design parameters and noise factors in the orthogonal arrays and to compute the signal-to-noise (SN) ratio based on the quality loss for each experimental combination.

OR

Experimental design is used in this method for arranging the design parameters and noise factors in the orthogonal arrays and for computing the signal-to-noise (SN) ratio based on the quality loss for each experimental combination.

6. The relative importance of each response can be transformed into a fuzzy number through means of the establishment of a formal scale system that can be used to convert linguistic terms into their corresponding fuzzy numbers and to express the relative importance of each response by the linguistic term.

The relative importance of each response can be transformed into a fuzzy number through means of establishing a formal scale system that can convert linguistic terms into their corresponding fuzzy numbers and express the relative importance of each response by the linguistic term.

EDITOR'S NOTE 4.4 Avoid wordiness by saying **by** instead of **through means of.**

7. The Taguchi approach provides a combination of experimental design
    techniques with quality loss considerations and that the average
    quadratic loss is minimized.

    The Taguchi combines experimental design techniques with quality loss considerations and minimizes the average quadratic loss.

8. The conventional approach happens to be cumbersome, complicated
    and wastes too much time.

    The conventional approach happens to be cumbersome, complicated and time consuming.

    EDITOR'S NOTE 4.5 Avoid wordiness by saying **is** instead of **happens to be.**

9. The two-step procedure not only identifies those factors that
    significantly affect the signal-to-noise (SN) ratio, but also the levels
    that maximize SN are found.

    The two-step procedure not only identifies those factors that significantly affect the signal-to-noise (SN) ratio, but also finds the levels that maximize SN.

10. Logethetis (1988) proved that strong non-linearities exist and the *B* technique was also recommended for use by him.

Logethetis (1988) proved that strong non-linearities exist and also recommended using the *B* technique.

> *EDITOR'S NOTE 4.6* Depending on the sentence's context, **demonstrated, verified,** or **confirmed** can be used as alternatives to **proved** when the Chinese meaning is 證明.

11. This work not only proposes an effective procedure based on the rank transformation of responses and regression analysis, but also the singly censored data are discussed.

This work not only proposes an effective procedure based on the rank transformation of responses and regression analysis, but also discusses the singly censored data.

> *EDITOR'S NOTE 4.7* Depending on the sentence's context, **presents** or **describes** can be used as alternatives to **proposes** when the Chinese meaning is 提出.

12. The following steps describe the procedure:

Step 1: Calculate the normalized decision matrix.

Step 2: The weighted normalized decision matrix is calculated.

Exercise 12

Step 3: The ideal and negative-ideal solution is determined.

Step 4: Calculate the separation measures.

Step 5: The relative closeness to the ideal solution is calculated.

Step 6: The preference order is ranked.

The following steps describe the procedure:

Step 1: Calculate the normalized decision matrix.

Step 2: Calculate the weighted normalized decision matrix.

Step 3: Determine the ideal and negative-ideal solution.

Step 4: Calculate the separation measures.

Step 5: Calculate the relative closeness to the ideal solution.

Step 6: Rank the preference order.

Exercise 13

Correct the following sentences using the copyediting marks on page 1.

1. Conventional approaches offer an explanation of this phenomenon and providing alternative strategies to solve the problem.

2. Their approach involves converting fuzzy data into crisp scores and to determine the ranking order of alternatives.

3. Crisp scores are assigned to the selected conversion scale (fuzzy number) for the purpose of applying a fuzzy scoring method and normalization of the scores.

4. The project concentrates mainly on reduction of the dependence between the sample mean and the sample standard deviation and that an efficient procedure capable of attaining the minimum quality loss is developed.

5. The standard procedure is for all intents and purposes inefficient, impractical, and creates problems.

6.   Ullman [1989] not only used the Analysis of Means (ANOM) to study

the mean response, but also a further extension of the ANOM was

made to analyze dispersion effects.

7.   The Taguchi Method deals with a one-dimensional problem and

multi-dimensional problems are handled by TOPSIS.

8.   The calculations are performed either to get a revised least squares fit

or expected failure times are estimated for the censored values.

9.   The proposed optimization procedure is made up of the following steps:

Step 1: Transform the relative importance of each response into a fuzzy

number.

Step 2: Crisp scores must be assigned to the selected conversion scale.

Step 3: The quality loss is computed.

Step 4: Determine the TOPSIS value for each trial.

Step 5: The optimal factor/level combination must be determined.

Step 6: The confirmation experiment is conducted.

10. Wee [11] made a further extension of the conventional model to allow for shortages and assuming that the demand rate would decrease exponentially.

11. The relative closeness computed in TOPSIS can be used to assess the performance measurement and optimizing multi-response problems in the Taguchi method.

12. The experiment focused on determination of how process parameters affect the silicon nitride deposition process and to satisfy the industrial requirements.

Answers
Exercise 13

1. Conventional approaches ~~offer an explanation of~~ this phenomenon and ~~providing~~ alternative strategies to solve the problem.

    Conventional approaches explain this phenomenon and provide alternative strategies to solve the problem

    > *EDITOR'S NOTE 4.8* Depending on the sentence's context, **alleviate, alter, modify, resolve, eliminate,** or **eradicate** can be used as alternatives to **solve** when the Chinese meaning is 解決. Also, depending on the sentence's context, **limitation, restriction, constraint,** or **phenomenon** can be used as an alternative to **problem** when the Chinese meaning is 問題.

2. Their approach ~~involves~~ converting fuzzy data into crisp scores and ~~to~~ determine the ranking order of alternatives.

    Their approach converts fuzzy data into crisp scores and determines the ranking order of alternatives.

3. Crisp scores are assigned to the selected conversion scale (fuzzy number) ~~for the purpose of~~ applying a fuzzy scoring method and normalization of the scores.

    Crisp scores are assigned to the selected conversion scale (fuzzy number) to apply a fuzzy scoring method and normalize the scores.

    > *EDITOR'S NOTE 4.9* Avoid wordiness by saying **for** or **to** instead of **for the purpose of.**

4.   The project concentrates mainly on reduction of the dependence between the sample mean and the sample standard deviation and that an efficient procedure capable of attaining the minimum quality loss is developed.

The project concentrates mainly on reducing the dependence between the sample mean and the sample standard deviation and developing an efficient procedure capable of attaining the minimum quality loss.

5.   The standard procedure is for all intents and purposes inefficient, impractical, and creates problems.

The standard procedure is for all intents and purposes inefficient, impractical, and problematic.

> ***EDITOR'S NOTE 4.10*** Omit needless phrases such as **for all intents and purposes** since they do not add to the sentence's overall meaning.

6.   Ullman [1989] not only used the Analysis of Means (ANOM) to study the mean response, but also a further extension of the ANOM was made to analyze dispersion effects.

Ullman [1989] not only used the Analysis of Means (ANOM) to study the mean response, but also further extended the ANOM to analyze dispersion effects.

Exercise 13

EDITOR'S NOTE 4.11 Depending on the sentence's context, **apply, employ,** or **utilize** can be used as alternatives to **use** when the Chinese meaning is 使用. Also, depending on the sentence's context, **investigate, examine, elucidate,** or **explore** can be used as alternatives to **study** when the Chinese meaning is 研究.

7.   The Taguchi Method deals with a one-dimensional problem and multi-dimensional problems are handled by TOPSIS.

The Taguchi Method deals with a one-dimensional problem and TOPSIS handles multi-dimensional problems.

8.   The calculations are performed either to get a revised least squares fit or expected failure times are estimated for the censored values.

The calculations are performed either to get a revised least squares fit or to estimate expected failure times for the censored values.

EDITOR'S NOTE 4.12 Depending on the sentence's context, **obtain, derive,** or **attain** can be used as alternatives to **get** when the Chinese meaning is 得到.

9.   The proposed optimization procedure is made up of the following steps:

Step 1: Transform the relative importance of each response into a fuzzy number.

Step 2: Crisp scores ~~must be~~ assigned to the selected conversion scale.

Step 3: The quality loss is computed.

Step 4: Determine the TOPSIS value for each trial.

Step 5: The optimal factor/level combination ~~must be~~ determined.

Step 6: The confirmation experiment is conducted.

The proposed optimization procedure is made of the following steps:

Step 1: Transform the relative importance of each response into a fuzzy number.

Step 2: Assign crisp scores to the selected conversion scale.

Step 3: Compute the quality loss.

Step 4: Determine the TOPSIS value for each trial.

Step 5: Determine the optimal factor/level combination.

Step 6: Conduct the confirmation experiment.

EDITOR'S NOTE 4.13 Depending on the sentence's context, **consists of** or **comprises of** can be used as alternatives to **is made up of** or **is made of** when the Chinese meaning is 由...做成.

10. Wee [11] made a further extension of the conventional model to allow

    for shortages and assuming that the demand rate would decrease

    exponentially.

    **Wee [11] further extended the conventional model to allow for shortages and
    assumed that the demand rate would decrease exponentially.**

11. The relative closeness computed in TOPSIS can be used to assess the

    performance measurement and optimizing multi-response problems in

    the Taguchi method.

    **The relative closeness computed in TOPSIS can be used to assess the perfor-
    mance measurement and optimize multi-response problems in the Taguchi
    method.**

    OR

    **The relative closeness computed in TOPSIS can be used for assessing the
    performance measurement and optimizing multi-response problems in the
    Taguchi method.**

12. The experiment focused on determination of how process parameters

    affect the silicon nitride deposition process and to satisfy the industrial

    requirements.

    **The experiment determined how process parameters affect the silicon nitride
    deposition process and, in doing so, satisfied the industrial requirements.**

Exercise 14

Correct the following sentences using the copyediting marks on page 1.

1. Yum and Ko [1] made a recommendation of starting with Taguchi's two-step procedure and that the transformation be applied in case (C1) is not satisfied.

2. The factors are in some cases identified, estimated, and easy for implementation.

3. Either the design factors should be examined or implementation of the two-step procedure should not be made.

4. The proposed procedure is simpler than conventional methods and analyzes an experiment with singly censored data.

5. The maximum likelihood method is not only frequently used by statisticians, but also those having limited statistical training find it difficult to comprehend.

6. Transforming the relative importance of each response into a fuzzy number consists of the following steps:

    (a) Express the relative importance of each response by a linguistic term.

    (b) A formal scale system is established that can be used to convert linguistic terms into their corresponding fuzzy numbers.

    (c) A conversion scale is found that matches all of the linguistic terms.

7. The numerical example concentrates mainly on illustration of the cases derived in the previous section and demonstrating the effectiveness of the proposed model.

8. The most frequent issues encountered in multi-response problems are resolving the conflict among responses, dealing with a different measurement unit for each response, and to assign a set of weights to the current information about the relative response of each problem.

9. The two responses can be optimized on the basis of determination of the optimal settings for factors B, C, D, E, F and G and to set factor A at level 1 and to set factor H at level 3.

10. The committee made a decision to set a new agenda and that the meeting should be adjourned.

11. The robust design focuses not only on collecting data accumulated from the designed experiment, but also that the results obtained by using Taguchi's two-step procedure are compared.

12. The proposed project is promising, creative, and has innovative ideas.

Answers

Exercise 14

1. Yum and Ko [1] ~~made a~~ recommend~~ation of~~ starting with Taguchi's

    two-step procedure and ~~that~~ the transformation be applied in case (C1)

    is not satisfied.

    Yum and Ko [1] recommended starting with Taguchi's two-step procedure
    and applied the transformation in case (C1) is not satisfied.

    EDITOR'S NOTE 4.14 Avoid wordiness by saying **if** instead of **in case.**

2. The factors are in some cases identified, estimated, and easy ~~for~~

    implement~~ation~~.

    The factors are in some cases identified, estimated, and easily implemented.

    EDITOR'S NOTE 4.15 Avoid wordiness by saying **occasionally** instead of **in some cases.**

3. Either the design factors should be examined or implement~~ation of~~ the

    two-step procedure should not be ~~made~~.

    Either the design factors should be examined or the two-step procedure
    should not be implemented.

4. The proposed procedure is simpler than conventional methods and analyzes an experiment with singly censored data.

Simpler than conventional methods, the proposed procedure analyzes an experiment with singly censored data.

OR

The proposed procedure, simpler than conventional methods, analyzes an experiment with singly censored data.

OR

The proposed procedure is simpler than conventional methods because it analyzes an experiment with singly censored data.

5. The maximum likelihood method is not only frequently used by statisticians, but also those having limited statistical training find it difficult to comprehend.

The maximum likelihood method is not only frequently used by statisticians, but also difficult to comprehend for those having limited statistical training.

6. Transforming the relative importance of each response into a fuzzy number consists of the following steps:

(a) Express the relative importance of each response by a linguistic term.

(b) A formal scale system is established that can convert linguistic terms into their corresponding fuzzy numbers.

Find

(c) A conversion scale is found that matches all of the linguistic terms.

Transforming the relative importance of each response into a fuzzy number consists of the following steps:

(a)   Express the relative importance of each response by the linguistic term.

(b)   Establish a formal scale system that can be used to convert linguistic terms into their corresponding fuzzy numbers.

(c)   Find a conversion scale that matches all of the linguistic terms.

7.   The numerical example concentrates mainly on illustration of the cases derived in the previous section and demonstrating the effectiveness of the proposed model.

The numerical example illustrates the cases derived in the previous section and demonstrates the effectiveness of the proposed model

OR

The numerical example concentrates mainly on illustrating the cases derived in the previous section and demonstrating the effectiveness of the proposed method.

8. The most frequent issues encountered in multi-response problems are resolving the conflict among responses, dealing with a different measurement unit for each response, and *~~to~~* assign*ing* a set of weights to the current information about the relative response of each problem.

The most frequent issues encountered in multi-response problems are resolving the conflict among responses, dealing with a different measurement unit for each response, and assigning a set of weights to the current information about the relative response of each problem.

> ***EDITOR'S NOTE 4.16*** Depending on the sentence's context, ***regarding, concerning,*** or ***involving*** can be used as alternatives to ***about*** when the Chinese meaning is 關於.

9. The two responses can be optimized on the basis of determin*~~ation of~~*ing the optimal settings for factors B, C, D, E, F and G *~~and to~~* *while* set*ting* factor A at level 1 and *~~to set~~* factor H at level 3.

The two responses can be optimized on the basis of determining the optimal settings for factors B, C, D, E, F and G, while setting factor A at level 1 and factor H at level 3.

> ***EDITOR'S NOTE 4.17*** Avoid wordiness by saying ***by, from,*** or ***because*** instead of ***on the basis of.*** In this sentence, ***by*** is the logical substitute.

10. The committee ~~made a~~ decision to set a new agenda and ~~that~~ the meeting ~~should be~~ adjourned.

The committee decided to set a new agenda and adjourn the meeting.

11. The robust design focuses not only on collecting data accumulated from the designed experiment, but also ~~that~~ the results obtained by using Taguchi's two-step procedure are compared.

The robust design focuses not only on collecting data accumulated from the designed experiment, but also on comparing the results obtained by using Taguchi's two-step procedure.

> **EDITOR'S NOTE 4.18** Depending on the sentence's context, **accumulating** and **gathering** can be used as alternatives to **collecting** when the Chinese meaning is 蒐集.

12. The proposed project is promising, creative, and ~~has~~ innovative ~~ideas~~.

The proposed project is promising, creative, and innovative.

Exercise 15

Correct the following sentences using the copyediting marks on page 1.

1. Incomplete data is commonly referred to as censored data and often occurs when the response variable is time to failure, e.g., accelerated life testing.

2. Their method suggested either using iterative least squares (ILS) to analyze censored data or the initial fit is used to estimate the expected failure time for each censored observation.

3. The TOPSIS value for each trial and the optimal factor/level combination can be determined in the following steps:

   Apply equations (4) ~ (8) to compute the relative closeness of each trial.

   The TOPSIS value in the ith trial is set to the designated value.

   The factor effects based on the TOPSIS value are estimated.

   Determine the optimal control factors and their levels.

4.   The systems manager is in no case responsible for combining the experimental design techniques with quality loss considerations and careful consideration of how the various factors affect performance variation.

5.   Herein, TOPSIS is applied to reduce the computational complexity, satisfy Taguchi's quality's loss, and finding a performance measurement index for each trial.

6.   The proposed procedure is employed for transformation of the relative importance of each response, to compute the quality loss, determination of the TOPSIS value, to select the optimal factor/level combination, and analysis of a confirmation experiment.

7.   The engineer makes an adjustment of the processing parameters and that the shop floor layout is finalized.

8.   The proposed mechanism is adaptive, flexible, efficient, and can be applied in a factory setting.

9. This section not only presents a numerical example, but also the effectiveness of the proposed GA-based procedure for cell formation problems is demonstrated.

10. The censored data contain less information than complete data and analysis is made more difficult to perform.

11. The proposed model not only performs diagnostic checking, but also the optimal factor/level combination is determined.

12. The procedure to determine the optimal factor/level combination in a multi-response problem is described as follows:

    Step 1: Estimate the factor effects.

    A. The factor effects are plotted and the main effects on MRSN are tabulated.

    B. Plot the factor efforts and tabulate the main effects on the mean response for the nominal-the-best case.

Step 2: The optimal control factors and their levels are determined.

A.   Find the control factor that significantly affects MRSN.

B.   The optimum level for each control factor is determined.

Step 3: The optimal adjustment factors are determined.

Answers
Exercise 15

1. Incomplete data is commonly referred to as censored data and often

   occurs when the response variable is time to failure, e.g., accelerated

   life testing.

   Incomplete data, commonly referred to as censored data, often occurs when

   the response variable is time to failure, e.g., accelerated life testing.

   OR

   Commonly referred to as censored data, incomplete data often occurs when

   the response variable is time to failure, e.g., accelerated life testing.

2. Their method suggested either using iterative least squares (ILS) to

   analyze censored data or the initial fit is used to estimate the expected

   failure time for each censored observation.

   Their method suggested using either iterative least squares (ILS) to analyze
   censored data or the initial fit to estimate the expected failure time for each
   censored observation.

3. The TOPSIS value for each trial and the optimal factor/level

   combination can be determined in the following steps:

Apply equations (4) ~ (8) to compute the relative closeness of each trial.

The TOPSIS value in the ith trial is set to the designated value.

The factor effects based on the TOPSIS value are estimated.

Determine the optimal control factors and their levels.

The TOPSIS value for each trial and the optimal factor/level combination can be determined in the following steps:

Apply equations (4) ~ (8) to compute the relative closeness of each trial.

Set the TOPSIS value in the ith trial to the designated value.

Estimate the factor effects based on TOPSIS value.

Determine the optimal control factors and their levels.

4.   The systems manager is in no case responsible for combining the experimental design techniques with quality loss considerations and careful consideration of how the various factors affect performance variation.

The systems manager is in no case responsible for combining the experimental design techniques with quality loss considerations and carefully considering how the various factors affect performance variation.

EDITOR'S NOTE 4.19 Avoid wordiness by saying **never** instead of **in no case.**

5. Herein, TOPSIS is applied to reduce the computational complexity, satisfy Taguchi's quality's loss, and finding a performance measurement index for each trial.

Herein, TOPSIS is applied to reduce the computational complexity, satisfy Taguchi's quality's loss, and find a performance measurement index for each trial.

6. The proposed procedure is employed for transformation of the relative importance of each response, to compute the quality loss, determination of the TOPSIS value, to select the optimal factor/level combination, and analysis of a confirmation experiment.

The proposed procedure is employed to transform the relative importance of each response, compute the quality loss, determine the TOPSIS value, select the optimal factor/level combination, and analyze a confirmation experiment.

7. The engineer makes an adjustment of the processing parameters and that the shop floor layout is finalized.

The engineer adjusts the processing parameters and finalizes the shop floor layout.

8.   The proposed mechanism is adaptive, flexible, efficient, and ~~can be~~
     cable
     applied in a factory setting.

The proposed mechanism is adaptive, flexible, efficient, and applicable in a factory setting.

9.   This section not only presents a numerical example, but also the

effectiveness of the proposed GA-based procedure for cell formation

problems is demonstrated.

This section not only presents a numerical example, but also demonstrates the effectiveness of the proposed GA-based procedure for cell formation problems.

10. The censored data contain less information than complete data and

analysis is made more difficult to perform.

The censored data contain less information than complete data and make analysis more difficult to perform.

OR

The censored data is less than complete, making analysis difficult to perform.

11. The proposed model not only performs diagnostic checking, but also the optimal factor/level combination is determined.

The proposed model not only performs diagnostic checking, but also determines the optimal factor/level combination.

12. The procedure to determine the optimal factor/level combination in a multi-response problem is described as follows:

Step 1: Estimate the factor effects.

A. The factor effects are plotted and the main effects on MRSN are tabulated.

B. Plot the factor efforts and tabulate the main effects on the mean response for the nominal-the-best case.

Step 2: The optimal control factors and their levels are determined.

A. Find the control factor that significantly affects MRSN.

Exercise 15

B. 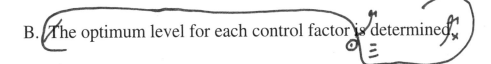 The optimum level for each control factor is determined.

Step 3: 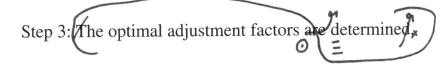 The optimal adjustment factors are determined.

The procedure to determine the optimal factor/level combination in a multi-response problem is described as follows:

Step 1: Estimate the factor effects.

A. Plot the factor effects and tabulate the main effects on MRSN.

B. Plot the factor efforts and tabulate the main effects on the mean response for the nominal-the-best case.

Step 2: Determine the optimal control factors and their levels.

A. Find the control factor that significantly affects MRSN.

B. Determine the optimum level for each control factor.

Step 3: Determine the optimal adjustment factors.

UNIT FIVE
Eliminate modifier problems

單元五 ： 去除修飾語所造成的問題

As a word, phrase, or clause, a modifier describes another word, phrase, or clause. The reader becomes confused when the modifying clause or phrase is not next to the word it modifies. This often creates a gap between the author's intended meaning and what is actually written.
修飾語必須放在所要修飾的字之旁。

Consider the following examples:

To effectively implement the policy, concrete measures must be adopt by the board of directors.

Logically, **concrete measures** can not **effectively implement the policy**. Therefore, placing the modifying clause next to what it modifies by switching from passive to active voice makes the intended meaning clear:

To effectively implement the policy, the board of directors must adopt concrete measures.

Placing the subject towards the front of the sentence makes the intended meaning even more direct:

The board of directors must adopt concrete measures to effectively implement the policy.

Consider another example of a modifier-related problem:

As an elementary student, my teacher taught me how to write Chinese characters.

Similar to the above example, **As an elementary student** mistakenly implies the subject of the sentence **my teacher**. The revision should read as

My elementary teacher taught me how to write Chinese characters.

A dangling modifier lacks the proper word in a sentence to modify, thereby making the sentence illogical.　Consider the following example:

Original

Being a complex formula, the statistician derived the equation with much precision.

Revised

Because the equation was a complex formula, the statistician derived it with much precision.

The following exercises provide further examples of modifier-related problems.

Exercise 16

Correct the following sentences using the copyediting marks on page 1.

1. To succeed in the laboratory, diligence is essential due to the fact that many experiments are necessary.

2. Before submitting a graduate school application, the institution should be selected.

3. Pressing the start button, the machine turned on.

4. While simulating the environment, the outcome yielded some surprising results.

5. The program contains the proposed itinerary that was implemented yesterday.

6. The container held by the experimenter with many leaks must be replaced.

7. To select the levels of the design parameter, the effects of the noise factors must be minimized.

8. Analyzing the SN ratios, the optimal settings can be determined.

9. When taking an examination, the questions should be answered as thoroughly as possible.

10. To excel in academics, determination is necessary.

11. While conducting an experiment, the timer went off and Jeff took the sample from the oven.

12. Taking into account all of the circumstances, the decision on how to deal with the issue was reached by the academic committee.

Answers

Exercise 16

the research must be

1. To succeed in the laboratory, diligence is essential due to the fact that many experiments are necessary.

To succeed in the laboratory, the researcher must be diligent due to the fact that many experiments are necessary.

OR

The researcher must be diligent to succeed in the laboratory due to the fact that many experiments are necessary.

EDITOR'S NOTE 5.1 Avoid wordiness by saying **because** or **since** instead of **due to the fact that**.

a student

2. Before submitting a graduate school application, the institution should be selected.

Before a student submits a graduate school application, the institution should be selected.

OR

A student should select the institute before submitting a graduate school application.

3. Pressing the start button prior to operations, the machine turned on.

The machine turned on after the operator pressed the start button.

OR

After the operator pressed the start button, the machine turned on.

OR (if you think that the action is more important than the doer of the action)

Pressing the start button turned the machine on.

4. When simulating the environment, the outcome yielded some surprising results.

When the laboratory assistant simulated the environment, the outcome yielded some surprising results.

EDITOR'S NOTE 5.2 Although the writer of this sentence implies that someone is *simulating the environment,* the reader will erroneously assume that the outcome is simulating the environment. The revised sentence eliminates this confusion.

5. The program contains the proposed itinerary that was implemented yesterday.

The program implemented yesterday contains the proposed itinerary.

EDITOR'S NOTE 5.3 In this sentence, although the writer wishes to state that what *was implemented yesterday* was *The program,* misplacing the clause changes the intended meaning.

6. The container held by the experimenter with many leaks must be replaced.

Held by the experimenter, the container with many leaks must be replaced.

The container held by the experimenter must be replaced owing to its many leaks.

> **EDITOR'S NOTE 5.4** Placing the modifying phrase in the wrong place erroneously states that *the experimenter,* not *The container,* has many leaks.

7. To select the levels of the design parameter, the effects of the noise factors must be minimized.

the engineer

To select the levels of the design parameter, the engineer must minimize the effects of the noise factors.

OR

The engineer must minimize the effects of the noise factors to select the levels of the design parameter.

8. Analyzing the SN ratios, the optimal settings can be determined.

by

The optimal settings can be determined by analyzing the SN ratios.

9. When taking an examination, (a student) the questions should be answered as

thoroughly as possible.

When taking an examination, a student should answer the questions as thoroughly as possible.

10. To excel in academics, determination is necessary.

Determination is necessary to excel in academics.

Or

For a student to excel in academics, determination is necessary.

11. While (Jeff was) conducting an experiment, the timer went off and Jeff (he) took the

sample from the oven.

While Jeff was conducting an experiment, the timer went off and he took the sample from the oven.

12. By Taking into account all of the circumstances, the decision on (decided) how to

deal with the issue was reached by the academic committee.

By taking into account all of the circumstances, the academic committee decided how to deal with the issue.

Or even better

The academic committee decided how to deal with the issue by taking all of the circumstances into account.

Exercise 17

Correct the following sentences using the copyediting marks on page 1.

1. Closely examining the test results, the final trial run was delayed by the laboratory manager for another two weeks.

2. He observed the phenomenon conducting the simulation run.

3. The technician detected the error analyzing the samples.

4. Having a large database, much information is contained in the system's network.

5. The technology has been advanced to satisfy consumer demand in recent years.

6. After considering the consumer reaction, which is volatile in the early stages of development, a decrease in production output was his decision.

7. When only seventeen years old, the university president granted her a doctorate degree.

8. To fully understand a lecture, note taking skills must be developed by the seminar participant.

9. When a research assistant, my colleague helped me conduct many experiments.

10. To calibrate the instruments, accuracy should be emphasized.

11. To measure the boundary parameters, precision must be incorporated.

12. When preparing for an interview, background information of that company should be researched.

Answers

Exercise 17

1. Closely examining the test results, the final trial was delayed by the

    laboratory manager for another two weeks.

    **Closely examining the test results, the laboratory manager delayed the final
    trial for another two weeks.**

    Or even better

    **The laboratory manager delayed the final trial for another two weeks after
    closely examining the test results.**

2. He observed the phenomenon conducting the simulation run.

    He observed the phenomenon while he was conducting the simulation run.

3. The technician detected the error analyzing the samples.

    While analyzing the samples, the technician detected the error.

    Or even better

    The technician detected the error while analyzing the samples.

4. Having a large database, much information is contained in the system's network.

Having a large database, the system's network contains much information.

Or even better

The system's network contains much information because it has a large database.

5. The technology has been advanced to satisfy consumer demand in recent years.

The technology has been advanced in recent years to satisfy consumer demand.

6. After considering the consumer reaction, which is volatile in the early stages of development, a decrease in production output was his decision.

After considering the consumer reaction, which is volatile in the early stages of development, he decided to decrease production output.

7. When only seventeen years old, the university president granted her a doctorate degree.

When she was only seventeen years old, the university president granted her a doctorate degree.

OR

The university president granted her a doctorate degree when she was only seventeen years old.

8.   To fully understand a lecture, note taking skills must be developed by the seminar participant.

To fully understand a lecture, the seminar participant must develop note taking skills.

OR

The seminar participant must develop note taking skills to fully understand a lecture.

9.   When *I was* a research assistant, my colleague helped me conduct many experiments.

My colleague helped me conduct many experiments when I was a research assistant.

OR

When I was a research assistant, my colleague helped me conduct many experiments.

10. To calibrate the instruments, *the technician* accuracy should be emphasized.

To calibrate the instruments, the technician should emphasize accuracy.

OR

The technician should emphasize accuracy when calibrating the instruments.

11. To measure the boundary parameters, precision must be incorporated.

The mathematician must incorporate precision when measuring the boundary parameters.

OR

To measure the boundary parameters, the mathematician must incorporate precision.

OR

The mathematician must be precise when measuring the boundary parameters.

12. When preparing for an interview, background information of that company should be researched.

When preparing for an interview, a job applicant should research background information of that company.

OR

A job applicant should research background information of that company when preparing for an interview.

Exercise 18

Correct the following sentences using the copyediting marks on page 1.

1. To keep in shape, exercise is a must for an athlete.

2. When an engineer, customer satisfaction should be attempted.

3. After simulating a real environment, a consensus was reached.

4. Being radioactive, the technician handled the materials with extreme

    care.

5. Several investigations calibrated errors related to camera distortion,

    which occurred in the 1990's.

6. The pedestrian warned the passing car with an angry look.

7. The cellular manufacturing system has been increasingly applied to

    industry, which is an important group technology application.

8. A genetic algorithm is appropriate for the machine-component grouping problem which is a robust adaptive optimization method based on principles of natural evolution.

9. To encourage adult literacy, public reading rooms have been established in the city.

10. When logging onto the Internet, complicated programming tasks are unnecessary.

11. As a child, my mother encouraged me to read many books.

12. Entering the apartment, the lights had been left on.

Answers

Exercise 18

1. To keep in shape, exercise is a must for an athlete.

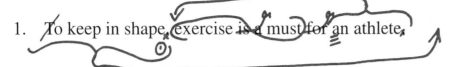

   An athlete must exercise to keep in shape.

2. When an engineer, customer satisfaction should be attempted.

   An engineer should attempt to satisfy the customer.

3. After simulating a real environment, a consensus was reached.

   After the researchers simulated a real environment, a consensus was reached.

4. Being radioactive, the technician handled the materials with extreme care.

   The technician handled the radioactive materials with extreme care.

5. Several investigations calibrated errors related to camera distortion, which occurred in the 1990's.

   Several investigations during the 1990's calibrated errors related to camera distortion.

6. The pedestrian warned the passing car with an angry look.

The pedestrian with an angry look warned the passing car.

> **EDITOR'S NOTE 5.5** It is illogical to state that *the passing car* has *an angry look.* The revised sentence eliminates the confusion.

7. The cellular manufacturing system has been increasingly applied to industry, which is an important group technology application.

The cellular manufacturing system, an important group technology application, has been increasingly applied to industry.

8. A genetic algorithm is appropriate for the machine-component grouping problem which is a robust adaptive optimization method based on principles of natural evolution.

Genetic algorithm, a robust adaptive optimization method based on principles of natural evolution, is appropriate for the machine-component grouping problem.

> **EDITOR'S NOTE 5.6** In this sentence, *a robust adaptive optimization method* illogically refers to *the machine-component grouping problem,* implying that the modifying clause has been misplaced. The revised sentence places the clause next to subject that it modifies.

Exercise 18

9.   To encourage adult literacy, public reading rooms have been established in

the city.

the government has

To encourage adult literacy, the government has established public reading rooms in the city.

Or even better

The government has established public reading rooms in the city to encourage adult literacy.

10. When logging onto the Internet, complicated programming tasks are

unnecessary.

Complicated programming tasks are unnecessary when logging onto the Internet.

OR

Logging onto the Internet does not require complicated programming tasks.

when I was

11. As a child, my mother encouraged me to read many books.

My mother encouraged me to read many books when I was a child.

I noticed that

12. Entering the apartment, the lights had been left on.

Entering the apartment, I noticed that the lights had been left on.

Exercise 19

Correct the following sentences using the copyediting marks on page 1.

1. Being made of concrete, the construction worker had difficulty in breaking the pavement.

2. Unable to pay their monthly bills, the finance company provided solutions for debt-ridden consumers.

3. After examining available options, feasible payment schedules were arranged by the financial consultant.

4. Registering for the fall semester, many elective courses were selected by the student.

5. Before moving into the student dormitory, full payment for the semester was required by the school.

6. As a computer instructor, students must be closely monitored.

7. To excel in academics, concentration skills must be developed.

8. To compensate the invited speaker for his participation, hotel accommodations and roundtrip airfare were provided by the conference committee.

9. When applying for graduate school admission, my academic advisor gave me valuable advice.

10. To make sound administrative decisions, many perspectives should be considered.

11. While scrolling down the screen, the monitor display suddenly turned off.

12. After attending the seminar that lasted all day, small group sessions were attended after dinner.

Answers
Exercise 19

1. ~~Being made of~~ concrete, the construction worker had difficulty in breaking the pavement.

    The construction worker had difficulty in breaking the concrete pavement.

2. Unable to pay their monthly bills, the finance company provided solutions for debt-ridden consumers.

    The finance company provided solutions for debt-ridden consumers unable to pay their monthly bills.

3. After examining available options, feasible payment schedules were arranged by the financial consultant.

    After examining available options, the financial consultant arranged feasible payment schedules.

    Or even better

    The financial consultant arranged feasible payment schedules after examining available options.

4. Registering for the fall semester, many elective courses were selected by the student.

when

The student selected many elective courses when registering for the fall semester.

5. Before moving into the student dormitory, full payment for the semester was required by the school.

one could

The school required full payment for the semester before one could move into the student dormitory.

6. As a computer instructor, students must be closely monitored.

A computer instructor must closely monitor students.

7. To excel in academics, concentration skills must be developed.

a student

To excel in academics, a student must develop concentration skills.

OR

A student must develop concentration skills to excel in academics.

8.　To compensate the invited speaker for his participation, hotel

accommodations and roundtrip airfare were provided by the conference committee.

To compensate the invited speaker for his participation, the conference committee provided hotel accommodations and roundtrip airfare.

OR

The conference committee provided the invited speaker with hotel accommodations and roundtrip airfare to compensate for his participation.

9.　When applying for graduate school admission, my academic advisor gave me valuable advice.

My academic advisor gave me valuable advice when I was applying for graduate school admission.

10.　To make sound administrative decisions, many perspectives should be considered.

A manager should consider many perspectives to make sound administrative decisions.

the computer user was

11. While scrolling down the screen, the monitor display suddenly turned

off.

**While the computer user was scrolling down the screen, the monitor display
suddenly turned off.**

12. After attending the seminar that lasted all day, small group sessions

participants

~~were~~ attended after dinner.

**After attending the seminar that lasted all day, participants attended small
group sessions after dinner.**

UNIT SIX
Double check for faulty comparisons and omissions

再次檢查錯誤的比較詞及粗心的疏漏

Sentences that contain comparisons that are illogical and incomplete create further ambiguity in technical writing. Editors must also recognize words that have been carelessly omitted.

不合邏輯及不完整的比較詞造成更多的含糊不清，同時注意不小心漏掉的字。

Consider the following examples:

The novel algorithm calculates the variables more efficiently.

In the sentence, **The novel algorithm calculates the variables more efficiently than** what? For clarity, the revised sentence should read as

The novel algorithm calculates the variables more efficiently than conventional ones.

Or consider another example of a faulty comparison:

The students respect the teacher more than the graduate assistant.

Depending the author's intended meaning, the revised sentence should read as

The students respect the teacher more than they respect the graduate student.

OR

The students prefer the teacher more than the graduate student does.

Consider two more examples:

Original
The new rules are as stringent, if not more stringent than, the old ones.
Revised
The new rules are as stringent as, if not more stringent than, the old ones.

Original
Their investigation thoroughly reviewed pertinent literature understand the physical phenomenon.

Revised
Their investigation thoroughly reviewed pertinent literature to understand the physical phenomenon.

The following exercises provide further examples of faulty comparisons and omissions.

Exercise 20

Correct the following sentences using the copyediting marks on page 1.

1. Our algorithm is more accurate with respect to computational time.

2. The chemistry department cooperates with local industry more than their department.

3. The novel material is as strong, if not stronger than, available ones.

4. The research department's productivity is higher than the administrative division.

5. The two step-procedure assumes that the sample standard deviation is proportional the sample mean.

6. The novel material described herein has a higher withstanding temperature.

7. The university stresses discipline more than the institute.

8. The peak is as high, if not higher than, other ones.

9. The form of the fitting function should be defined in advance adopt the regression method effectively.

10. The trade school's dropout rate is lower than the university.

11. Temperature more significantly affects the product's shape.

12. Our laboratory manager emphasizes punctuality more than our division director.

Answers

Exercise 20

1.   Our algorithm is more accurate with respect to computational time.

   Our algorithm is more accurate than conventional ones with respect to computational time.

2.   The chemistry department cooperates with local industry more than their department *does.*

   The chemistry department cooperates with local industry more than their department does.

3.   The novel material is as strong, if not stronger than, available ones.

   The novel material is as strong as, if not stronger than, available ones.

4.   The research department's productivity is higher than *that of* the administrative division.

   The research department's productivity is higher than that of the administrative division.

5. The two step-procedure assumes that the sample standard deviation is proportional to the sample mean.

    The two step-procedure assumes that the sample standard deviation is proportional to the sample mean.

6. The novel material described herein has a higher withstanding temperature than other materials.

    The novel material described herein has a higher withstanding temperature than other materials.

7. The university stresses discipline more than the institute does so.

    The university stresses discipline more than the institute does.

8. The peak is as high as, if not higher than, other ones.

    The peak is as high as, if not higher than, other ones.

9. The form of the fitting function should be defined in advance adopt the regression method to effectively.

    The form of the fitting function should be defined in advance to effectively adopt the regression method.

10   The trade school's dropout rate is lower than ~~that of~~ the university.

The trade school's dropout rate is lower than that of the university.

11.   Temperature ~~more~~ significantly affects the product's shape _than other factors_.

Temperature significantly affects the product's shape more than other factors.

12.   Our laboratory manager emphasizes punctuality more than our division director _does_.

Our laboratory manager emphasizes punctuality more than our division director does.

Exercise 21

Correct the following sentences using the copyediting marks on page 1.

1. State universities are as competitive, if not more competitive than, private ones.

2. A GA-based procedure is proposed solving the MCG problem.

3. During an earthquake, high rise apartment buildings are as safe, if not safer than, conventional housing.

4. Smith et al. (1) more thoroughly investigated the physical phenomenon.

5. The new curriculum emphasizes more practice than the old one.

6. The enrollment at the university is as high, if not higher than, at the institute.

7.   CM strives attain the benefits of a product-oriented layout.

8.   The temperature's decrease is slower than the height.

9.   Kaiser et al. (5) more thoroughly described the fusion reaction.

10.   I respect the teacher more than him.

11.   The CF method is as reliable, if not more reliable than, THI method.

12.   C&C analysis is only appropriate for parts that easily recognized.

Answers
Exercise 21

1. State universities are as competitive, if not more competitive than, private ones.

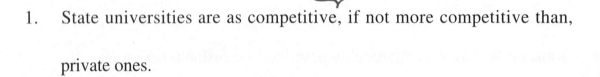

   State universities are as competitive as, if not more competitive than, private ones.

2. A GA-based procedure is proposed solving the MCG problem.

   A GA-based procedure is proposed for solving the MCG problem.

   OR

   A GA-based procedure is proposed to solve the MCG problem.

3. During an earthquake, high rise apartment buildings are as safe, if not safer than, conventional housing.

   During an earthquake, high rise apartment buildings are as safe as, if not safer than, conventional housing.

4. Smith et al. (1) more thoroughly investigated the physical phenomenon.

   Smith et al. (1) more thoroughly investigated the physical phenomenon than other researchers.

5.   The new curriculum emphasizes more practice than the old one. *does so*

The new curriculum emphasizes practice more than the old one does.

6.   The enrollment at the university is as high, *as* if not higher than, at the

institute.

The enrollment at the university is as high as, if not higher than, at the

institute.

7.   CM strives *to* attain the benefits of a product-oriented layout.

CM strives to attain the benefits of a product-oriented layout.

8.   The temperature's decrease is slower than *that of* the height.

The temperature's decrease is slower than that of the height.

9.   Kaiser et al. (5) more thoroughly described the fusion reaction. *than other researchers.*

Kaiser et al. (5) more thoroughly described the fusion reaction than other

researchers.

10. I respect the teacher more than him. _he does._

   I respect the teacher more than he does.

   OR

   I respect the teacher more than I admire him.

11. The CF method is as reliable _as_, if not more reliable than, THI method.

   CF method is as reliable as, if not more reliable than, THI method.

12. C&C analysis is only appropriate for parts that _are_ easily recognized.

   C&C analysis is only appropriate for parts that are easily recognized.

Exercise 22

Correct the following sentences using the copyediting marks on page 1.

1. An Internet company's success rate is lower than an electronics firm.

2. An ink jet printer is normally less expensive.

3. Listening is as important, if not important than, taking notes when attending a lecture.

4. Flat display monitors have as long a product life, if not longer than, normal ones.

5.   A graduate student's likelihood of securing employment when completing studies is higher than a university student.

6. Injuries incurred from playing football are usually more severe.

7. A machine's capacity to produce parts is greater than a worker.

8. School tuition can be as expensive, if not more expensive than, living expenses.

9. Venugopal and Narendran (1992b) considered limitations machine capacities, production amounts and processing times of parts.

10. SN ratios are analyzed determine the optimal settings of the design parameters.

11. A doctorate degree is usually more time consuming.

Answers

Exercise 22

1. An Internet company's success rate is lower than ~~that of~~ an electronics firm.

    An Internet company's success rate is lower than that of an electronics firm.

2. An ink jet printer is normally less expensive ~~than a laser one.~~

    An ink jet printer is normally less expensive than a laser one.

3. Listening is as important ~~as~~, if not important than, taking notes when

    attending a lecture.

    **Listening is as important as, if not more important than, taking notes when
    attending a lecture.**

4. Flat display monitors have as long a product life ~~as~~, if not longer than,

    normal ones.

    **Flat display monitors have as long a product life as, if not longer than, normal
    ones.**

5. A graduate student's likelihood of securing employment when completing studies is higher than ~~a~~ *that of* a university student.

    A graduate student's likelihood of securing employment when completing studies is higher than that of a university student.

    OR

    A graduate student is more likely to secure employment when completing studies than a university student.

6. Injuries incurred from playing football are usually more severe. *than those from other sports.*

    Injuries incurred from playing football are usually more severe than those from other sports.

7. A machine's capacity to produce parts is greater than *that of* a worker.

    A machine's capacity to produce parts is greater than that of a worker.

    OR

    A machine can produce parts better than a worker can.

8. School tuition can be as expensive *as*, if not more expensive than, living expenses.

    School tuition can be as expensive as, if not more expensive than, living expenses.

9. Venugopal and Narendran (1992b) considered limitations *of* machine capacities, production amounts and processing times of parts.

Venugopal and Narendran (1992b) considered limitations of machine capacities, production amounts and processing times of parts.

10. SN ratios are analyzed *to* determine the optimal settings of the design parameters.

SN ratios are analyzed to determine the optimal settings of the design parameters.

11. A doctorate degree is usually more time consuming *than other degrees.*

A doctorate degree is usually more time consuming than other degrees.

Exercise 23

Correct the following sentences using the copyediting marks on page 1.

1. A department director's authority is more powerful than an assistant.

2. Projected expenses can be as high, if not higher than, actual ones.

3. Hsinchu has a higher concentration of technical companies than any other in Taiwan.

4. Those objectives generally conflict each other.

5. Writing a rough draft can take longer.

6. Engineering judgement is used primarily solving the optimization of complicated multi-response problem in Taguchi's Method.

7. Expectations can be as great, if not greater than, one's ability.

8.   The rest of this paper organized as follows.

9.   Simultaneously optimizing different objectives a relatively difficult

task.

10.   This finding confirms that the proposed schemes are more efficient.

11.   The normalized value can be as large, if not larger than, that of the

quality loss.

12.   A researcher's salary can be as high, if not higher than, that of a

professor.

Answers

Exercise 23

1. A department director's authority is more powerful than ~~an~~ assistant. *that of*

   A department director's authority is more powerful than that of an

   assistant.

   OR

   A department director has more authority than an assistant does.

2. Projected expenses can be as high, if not higher than, actual ones. *as*

   Projected expenses can be as high as, if not higher than, actual ones.

3. Hsinchu has a higher concentration of technical companies than any other in Taiwan. *city*

   Hsinchu has a higher concentration of technical companies than any other city
   in Taiwan.

4. Those objectives generally conflict each other. *with*

   Those objectives generally conflict with each other.

Exercise 23

5. Writing a rough draft can take longer~~,~~ *than writing the final paper.*

Writing a rough draft can take longer than writing the final paper.

6. Engineering judgement is used primarily *for* solving the optimization of

complicated multi-response problem in Taguchi's Method.

Engineering judgement is used primarily for solving the optimization of complicated multi-response problems in Taguchi's Method.

7. Expectations can be as great, *as* if not greater than, one's ability.

Expectations can be as great as, if not greater than, one's ability.

8. The rest of this paper *is* organized as follows.

The rest of this paper is organized as follows.

9. Simultaneously optimizing different objectives *is* a relatively difficult

task.

Simultaneously optimizing different objectives is a relatively difficult task.

10. This finding confirms that the proposed schemes are more efficient~~,~~ *than conventional ones.*

This finding confirms that the proposed schemes are more efficient than conventional ones.

11. The normalized value can be as large *as*, if not larger than, that of the quality loss.

   The normalized value can be as large as, if not larger than, that of the quality loss.

12. A researcher's salary can be as high *as*, if not higher than, that of a professor.

   A researcher's salary can be as high as, if not higher than, that of a professor.

UNIT SEVEN
Avoid unnecessary shifts in a sentence

單元七 ：避完不必要的句中轉換

Another obstacle to clarity in technical writing is unnecessary shifts in subject, tense, voice and mood.
作者應避免句中不必要的主詞、時態及語態之轉換。

Consider the following examples:

When a computer user is finished writing a program, you should shut down the system properly.

The editor should avoid shifts from Third Person to First Person, or vice versa. The revised sentence should read as

When a computer user is finished writing a program, he or she should shut down the system properly.

OR

When a computer user is finished writing a program, the system should be shut down properly.

Another problem is when the writer shifts in number. Consider the following example:

Original
The secretary prefers using a laser jet printer instead of an ink jet printer because they produce a finer quality print.
Revised
The secretary prefers using a laser jet printer instead of an ink jet printer because it produces a finer quality print.

Yet another unnecessary shift in a sentence is when the writer changes verb tense. Consider the following example:

Original
The laboratory assistant performed the experiment and then summarizes her findings.
Revised
The laboratory assistant performed the experiment and then summarized her findings.

However, a shift in verb tense is necessary if the author is stating a fact, situation or assumption. Consider the following example:

Original
Wu (2000) thoroughly reviewed technology trends within the telecommunications industry, indicating that research involving broad bandwidths was increasing.
Revised
Wu (2000) thoroughly reviewed technology trends within the telecommunications industry, indicating that research involving broad bandwidths is increasing.

In the above example, **research involving broad bandwidths is increasing** is a fact. Therefore, the verb should be **is** instead of **was**. In this case, it is proper to shift tenses.

The following exercises provide further examples of unnecessary shifts within a sentence.

Exercise 24

Correct the following sentences using the copyediting marks on page 1.

1. When a student is preparing for an examination, you should get plenty
    of rest before the test despite the fact that intelligence plays a major
    role.

2. The graduate student recorded the data and then writes a summary
    report.

3. Turn on the machine if conditions are such that a hazard might occur
    and the valve should be closed.

4. It is noted that the academic advisor asked the graduate student if the
    paper was completed and is it ready to send to the journal for review.

5. It is interesting that the laboratory manager arranged the meeting and
    the discussion was led by him.

6.　It is possible that the researcher completes the experiment when you can not obtain any more valid results.

7.　The architect gives each program its separate address space and, in doing so, prevented an error that causes one program to fail from interfering with other programs running concurrently.

8.　The consumer realizes that the trackball is the ideal choice to make when they purchase a user interface of this type.

9.　Execute the necessary commands provided that they are valid and the program should be reviewed.

10.　The manager instructed the employees to arrange the final details and also is the final program ready to print.

11.　The speaker commented on the importance of participating in international events and then the meeting was adjourned by him.

Answers

Exercise 24

1. When a student is preparing for an examination, ~~you~~ *he or she* should get plenty

    of rest before the test despite the fact that intelligence plays a major

    role.

    **When a student is preparing for an examination, he or she should get plenty
    of rest   before the test despite the fact that intelligence plays a major role.**

    OR

    **A student should get plenty of rest when preparing for an examination despite
    the fact that intelligence plays a major role.**

    EDITOR'S NOTE 7.1 The writer should avoid shifting from Third Person to First Person, or vice versa.
    The writer should also avoid shifting from First Person to Second Person. Consider the following
    example:

    > *Original*
    > *I will not go to a coffee shop where you can not use the shop's electrical outlet for your
    > notebook computer.*
    > *Revised*
    > *I will not go to a coffee shop where I can not use the shop's electrical outlet for my
    > notebook computer.*

    EDITOR'S NOTE 7.2 Avoid wordiness by saying **although** instead of **despite the fact that.**

2. The graduate student recorded the data and then ~~writes~~ *wrote* a summary report.

The graduate student recorded the data and then wrote a summary report.

EDITOR'S NOTE 7.3 Shifting verb tense in a sentence is undesirable. However, a shift in verb tense is acceptable if the writer refers to something that occurred in the past, but then states a fact, finding, observation or assumption based on this previous event. Consider the following example:

Tsai and Li[2] *examined t*he factors that influence thermal stability, indicating that temperature *plays* a prominent role.

However, this example is the exception not the rule. Unnecessary shifts in verb tense should be avoided.

3. Turn on the machine if conditions are such that a hazard might occur and the valve ~~should be~~ closed.

Turn on the machine and close the valve if conditions are such that a hazard might occur.

EDITOR'S NOTE 7.4 The writer should avoid shifting moods, particularly from imperative (i.e., stating a command) to indicative (i.e., stating a fact or question).

EDITOR'S NOTE 7.5 Avoid wordiness by saying **if** instead of **if conditions are such that.**

4. It is noted that the academic advisor asked the graduate student if the paper was completed and ~~is it~~ ready to send to the journal for review.

It is noted that the academic advisor asked the graduate student if the paper was completed and ready to send to the journal for review.

> *EDITOR'S NOTE 7.6* The writer should avoid shifting from indirect course (i.e., reporting what the speaker said) to direct course(i.e., stating the actual words of the speaker), or vice versa.

> *EDITOR'S NOTE 7.7* Omit wordiness by saying **Notably,** instead of **It is noted that**; otherwise, omit the expression if unnecessary.

5. It is interesting that the laboratory manager arranged the meeting and

the discussion was led by him.

It is interesting that the laboratory manager arranged the meeting and led the discussion.

> *EDITOR'S NOTE 7.8* In the sentence, shifting the subject from **laboratory manager** to **discussion** makes the sentence less emphatic and confuses the reader from identifying the important subject.

> *EDITOR'S NOTE 7.9* Avoid wordiness by saying **Interestingly**, instead of **It is interesting that**; otherwise, omit the expression if unnecessary.

6. It is possible that the researcher completes the experiment when you *he or she*

can not obtain any more valid results.

It is possible that the researcher completes the experiment when he or she can not obtain any more valid results.

> *EDITOR'S NOTE 7.10* Avoid wordiness by saying *may, might, could,* or *can* instead of *It is possible that.*

7.　The architect gives each program its separate address space and, in doing so, prevented an error that causes one program to fail from interfering with other programs running concurrently.

The architect gives each program its separate address space and, in doing so, prevents an error that causes one program to fail from interfering with other programs running concurrently.

OR

The architect allots a separate address space for each program to prevent interference with other concurrent programs.

8.　The consumer realizes that the trackball is the ideal choice to make when they purchase a user interface of this type.

The consumer realizes that the trackball is the ideal choice to make when purchasing a user interface of this type.

9.　Execute the necessary commands provided that they are valid and the

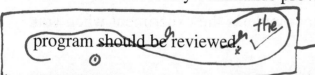

program should be reviewed.

Execute the necessary commands provided that they are valid and review the program.

> *EDITOR'S NOTE 7.11* Avoid wordiness by saying **if** instead of **provided that.**

10. The manager instructed the employees to arrange the final details and ~~asked~~

~~also is~~ *if* the final program *was* ready to print.

The manager instructed the employees to arrange the final and also asked if the final program was ready to print.

11. The speaker commented on the importance of participating in

international events and then the meeting was adjourned by him.

The speaker commented on the importance of participating in international events and then adjourned the meeting.

Exercise 25

Correct the following sentences using the copyediting marks on page 1.

1. When the engineer attempts to confirm prediction accuracy, you should not neglect possible errors.

2. An application makes calls to the executive kernel services, which will then make calls to the hardware.

3. Mice and trackballs are used for the same reason and it performs the same task.

4. Orient the new employees on factory floor procedures and they should be warned about potential workplace hazards.

5. Give consideration to the external factors and the surrounding environment must be assessed.

6. The web server makes an inquiry regarding the number of users and does the system become overloaded during evening hours.

7. The network programmer establishes a link between two or more

    people so you can exchange information.

8. The 100 Mbps Network Card is rapidly becoming the industrial standard

    for local area networks worldwide and had a per unit cost of around

    $110.

9. Not only can the devices be used to copy CDs in case of damage to

    the original, but it can also be used for backing up hard drives.

10. Ascertain the location of the missing value and the equation should be

    derived.

11. The student applied for a library card and could it be ready next week.

12. The organizing committee held the conference and invited speakers

    were compensated by it.

Answers
Exercise 25

1. When the engineer attempts to confirm prediction accuracy, ~~you~~ *he or she* should not neglect possible errors.

   When the engineer attempts to confirm prediction accuracy, he or she should not neglect possible errors.

   OR

   An engineer should not neglect possible errors when attempting to confirm prediction accuracy.

2. An application makes calls to the executive kernel services, which ~~will~~ then make*s* calls to the hardware.

   An application makes calls to the executive kernel services, which then makes calls to the hardware.

3. Mice and trackballs are used for the same reason and ~~it performs the~~ same task.

   Mice and trackballs are used for the same reason and perform the same task.

4. Orient the new employees on factory floor procedures and ~~they should~~ *them* ~~be~~ warned about potential workplace hazards.

Orient the new employees on factory floor procedures and warn them about potential workplace hazards.

5.   Give consideration to the external factors and the surrounding environment must be assessed.

Give consideration to the external factors and assess the surrounding environment.

> *EDITOR'S NOTE 7.12* Avoid wordiness hiding a verb inside of a noun. In this sentence, wordiness can be omitted by saying *Consider* instead of *Give consideration to.* Sentences can often be simplified by identifying verbs hiddent inside of nouns.

6.   The web server makes an inquiry regarding the number of users and does the system become overloaded during evening hours.

The web server makes an inquiry regarding the number of users and system overloading during evening hours.

> *EDITOR'S NOTE 7.13* Avoid wordiness by not overusing verbs such as *make, give, come, take, is, are, was, and were.* This sentence can also say asks about or inquires about instead of *makes an inquiry.*

7.   The network programmer establishes a link between two or more people so you can exchange information.

The network programmer establishes a link between two or more people to exchange information.

8. The 100 Mbps Network Card is rapidly becoming the industrial standard for local area networks worldwide and had a per unit cost of around $110.

    The 100 Mbps Network Card is rapidly becoming the industrial standard for local area networks worldwide and has a per unit cost of around $110.

    OR

    The 100 Mbps Network Card is rapidly becoming the industrial standard for local area networks worldwide with a unit cost of around $100.

9. Not only can the devices be used to copy CDs in case of damage to the original, but it can also be used for backing up hard drives.

    Not only can the devices copy CDs in case of damage to the original, but they can also back up hard drives.

    OR

    In addition to copying CDs in case of damage to the original, the devices can back up hard drives.

10. Ascertain the location of the missing value and the equation should be derived.

Ascertain the location of the missing value and, in doing so, derive the
equation.

> **EDITOR'S NOTE 7.14** Avoid wordiness by saying **Find** instead of **Ascertain the location of.**

> **EDITOR'S NOTE 7.15** Depending on the sentence's context, **obtain, derive, attain, locate,** and **identify** can be used as alternatives to **find**.

11. The student applied for a library card and ~~could~~ asked whether it would be ready next week.

    The student applied for a library card and asked whether it would be

    ready next week.

12. The organizing committee held the conference and invited speakers ~~were compensated by it.~~

    The organizing committee held the conference and compensated invited

    speakers.

Exercise 26

Correct the following sentences using the copyediting marks on page 1.

1. Communicators must share a common language or protocol so that we can easily understand each other.

2. A computer mouse needs some available workspace and even the beginning user can operate them with very little difficulty.

3. Execute the program commands and the iteration steps must be repeated.

4. The supervisor asked her employees if the assignment was ready and could it be handed in tomorrow.

5. The instructor made the class assignment and a follow up quiz was given by him .

6. For the user to clean the inside of a keyboard, you must remove the

    screws on the back of the keyboard with a very small screwdriver.

7. The rewritable recorder is designed to use one CD over and over and

    cost approximately $400.

8. The consumer should know the pros and cons of a compact disk

    recorder when purchasing them.

9. The company decided to update the operating systems on the

    engineering department computers so they can more easily access the

    mainframe.

10. The lecturer indicated that the role of telecommunications

    was increasingly common in daily life.

11. The new cartridges are large and should last a long time, making it

    more attractive than the older ones.

12. The college will purchase more computers in the near future so that you can communicate with your teachers on-line.

13. Space is needed to allow movement since a mouse is needed to move to perform its functions.

14. Netscape Navigator allows the e-mail user to access their accounts from anywhere in the world.

Answers

Exercise 26

1. Communicators must share a common language or protocol so that ~~we~~ *they* can easily understand each other.

    Communicators must share a common language or protocol so that they can easily understand each other.

2. A computer mouse needs some available workspace and even the beginning user can operate ~~them~~ *one* with very little difficulty.

    A computer mouse needs some available workspace and even the beginning user can operate one with very little difficulty.

3. Execute the program commands and the iteration steps ~~must be repeated~~.

    Execute the program commands and repeat the iteration steps.

4. The supervisor asked her employees if the assignment was ready and could ~~it~~ be handed in tomorrow.

    The supervisor asked her employees if the assignment was ready and could be handed in tomorrow.

    OR

The supervisor asked her employees if the assignment was ready to be handed in tomorrow.

5.   The instructor made the class assignment and ~~a follow up quiz was~~ gave a follow up quiz.

~~given by him.~~

The instructor made the class assignment and gave a follow up quiz.

6.   For the user to clean the inside of a keyboard, ~~you~~ he or she must remove the screws on the back of the keyboard with a very small screwdriver.

For the user to clean the inside of a keyboard, he or she must remove the screws on the back of the keyboard with a very small screwdriver.

OR even better

The user can clean the inside of a keyboard by removing the screws on the back with a very small screwdriver.

7.   The rewritable recorder is designed to use one CD over and over and costs approximately $400.

The re-rewirtable recorder is designed to use one CD over and over and costs approximately $400.

OR

The re-writable recorder is designed for one CD to be reused and costs approximately $400.

8.   The consumer should know the pros and cons of a compact disk

recorder when purchasing ~~them~~. *one*

The consumer should know the pros and cons of a compact disk recorder
when purchasing one.

9.   The company decided to update the operating systems on the

engineering department computers so th~~ey~~ can more easily access the *engineers*

mainframe.

The company decided to update the operating systems on the engineering
department computers so the engineers can more easily access the mainframe.

OR

The company decided toupdate the operating system on the engineering
department computers to more easily access the mainframe.

10.   The lecturer indicated that the role of telecommunications

~~was~~ increasingly common in daily life. *is*

The lecturer indicated that the role of telecommunications is increasingly
common in daily life.

EDITOR'S NOTE 7.16 Although it is important to maintain a consistent verb tense, one exception to
the rule is when the writer is stating a fact, situation or assumption. Since ***telecommunications in daily***
life is increasingly common is a fact, present tense should be used. Under this circumstance, shifting
verb tenses in a sentence is acceptable.

11. The new cartridges are large and should last a long time, making ~~it~~ *them*
more attractive than the older ones.

**The new cartridges are large and should last a long time, making them more
attractive than the older ones.**

12. The college will purchase more computers in the near future so that
students ~~you~~ can communicate with your teachers on-line.

**The college will purchase more computers in the near future so that students
can communicate with their teachers on-line.**

13. Space is needed to allow movement since a mouse ~~is~~ need*s* to move to
perform its functions.

**Space is needed to allow movement since a mouse needs to move to perform its
functions.**
OR
Space is needed to allow a mouse to perform its functions.

14. Netscape Navigator allows ~~the~~ e-mail user*s* to access their
accounts from anywhere around the world.

**Netscape Navigator allows e-mail users to access their accounts from any-
where around the world.**

UNIT EIGHT
Combine conciseness and clarity

單元八 ： 結合 " 精確寫作 " 及 " 明白寫作 "

Review conciseness

In addition to editing for **clarity**, the writer must also edit for **conciseness** to ensure that a manuscript is thoroughly revised. In the fourth book of *The Chinese Technical Writer Series*, <u>An Editing Workbook for Chinese Technical Writers</u>, emphasis was placed on editing for **conciseness**: how to refine an author's intended meaning by omitting stylistic errors that prevent him or her from writing succinct sentences. The following exercises review general principles of concise writing so that the writer can incorporate conciseness and clarity when editing his or her manuscript.

科技英文寫作系列之四 -- " 科技英文編修訓練手冊 " 強調精確寫作，即如何去除寫作格式錯誤，使作者的意思更為精簡。以下的練習題幫助您複習精確寫作的一般通則，以期可以和本書的明白寫作呵成一氣。

Exercise 27

Correct the following sentences by using the copyediting marks on page 1.

1. Modification of environmental technologies transferred from abroad for the local industrial sector is performed by the research institute.

2. Accurate prediction of the boundary parameters by mathematicians is of heavy emphasis.

3. An outline of how to install the software program is made in the following section.

4. A more thorough description of the environmental impact on the ozone layer was made by Smith (1985).

5. Contributing factors to rainforest depletion include overpopulation.

6. Awareness of external factors that contribute to industrial pollution must be known by the urban planner.

Exercise 27

7. No significant variation between the two temperatures occurred.

8. It is impossible to forecast all potential workplace hazards.

9. There is no need for the assessment of the production capacity of the factory floor to be undertaken by the foreman.

10. Carpooling can be arranged by means of a designated driver if conditions are such that commuters to the same workplace live in close proximity to each other.

11. A definite decision about future plans should not be made until a major breakthrough in product development occurs.

12. It is well known that telecommunications technologies happen to be expanding rapidly for the purpose of satisfying the growing consumer demand.

Answers

Exercise 27

1. Modification of environmental technologies transferred from abroad for the local industrial sector is performed by the research institute.

The research institute modifies environmental technology transferred from abroad for the local industrial sector.

EDITOR'S NOTE 8.1 Switching from passive voice to active voice makes this sentence more direct, concise and persuasive.

2. Accurate prediction of the boundary parameters by the mathematicians is of heavy emphasis.

The mathematicians heavily emphasize accurately predicting the boundary parameters.

EDITOR'S NOTE 8.2 Like in the previous sentence, using passive voice makes the sentence wordy or indecisive. However, active voice makes the sentence more direct and clear.

3. An outline of how to install the software program is made in the following section.

The following section outlines how to install the software program.

OR

The following section outlines the installation of the software program.

EDITOR'S NOTE 8.3 Using a verb instead of a noun simplifies this sentence. Avoid sentences that contain phrases like *is made, is done, is performed, is conducted, is undertaken* and *is achieved.* Such phrases often make the sentence unnecessarily long. Consider the following examples:

> **Original**
> **Simulation of the program is done.**
> **Revised**
> **The program is simulated.**
> **Original**
> **Implementation of the program is performed.**
> **Revised**
> **The program is implemented.**
> **Original**
> **Optimization of the output is achieved.**
> **Revised**
> **The output is optimized.**

4. A more thorough description of the environmental impact on the ozone layer was made by Smith (1985).

Smith (1985) more thoroughly described the environmental impact on the ozone layer.

5. Contributing factors to rainforest depletion include overpopulation.

Overpopulation contributes to rainforest depletion.

EDITOR'S NOTE 8.4 A writer should use strong verbs that imply a precise action. In this case, *contributes* implies a more precise action than *include.* Avoid overusing verbs like *make, come, take, is, are, was,* and *were* which often have a general meaning rather than a precise one. Consider the following examples:

> **Original (Unclear action)**
> **The purpose of this study is to understand the underlying factors.**
> **Revised (Clear action)**
> **This study attempts (aims) to understand the underlying factors.**

> **Original (Unclear action)**
> The committee made a decision on what to do next.
> **Revised (Clear action)**
> The committee decided what to do next.

6. Awareness of external factors that contribute to industrial pollution must be known by the urban planner.

   The urban planner must be aware of external factors that contribute to industrial pollution.

7. No significant variation between the two temperatures occurred.

   The two temperatures did not significantly vary.

8. It is impossible to forecast all potential workplace hazards.

   All potential workplace hazards can not be forecasted.

> **EDITOR'S NOTE 8.5** Writers should try to avoid sentences that start with **It** and **There** to save space and to achieve a greater emphasis. Consider the following examples:
>
> > **Original**
> > There are many programs available in Taiwan.
> > **Revised**
> > Many programs are available in Taiwan.
> > **Original**
> > It is possible to create many designs with the software.
> > **Revised**
> > The software can create many designs.
> > **OR**
> > **Revised**
> > Many designs can be created with the software.

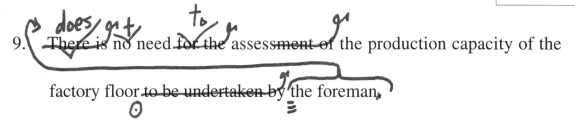

9. There is no need for the assessment of the production capacity of the factory floor to be undertaken by the foreman.

The foreman does not need to assess the production capacity of the factory floor.

> *EDITOR'S NOTE 8.6*   In this revised sentence, not only does the writer avoid the **There is** sentence opener but also turns a noun (**assessment**) into a verb (**assess**), thus shortening the sentence.

10. Carpooling can be arranged by means of a designated driver if conditions are such that commuters to the same workplace live in near close proximity to each other.

Carpooling can be arranged by a designated driver if commuters to the same workplace live near each other.

> *EDITOR'S NOTE 8.7*   The writer should try to avoid needless and redundant words and phrases that only make the sentence lengthy. Replacing *if conditions are such that* with *if* and *in close proximity* with *near* greatly simplifies the sentence. Unit Six of <u>An Editing Workbook for Chinese Technical Writers</u> provides more examples of needless and redundant words and phrases.

11. A definite decision about future plans should not be made until a major breakthrough in product development occurs.

A decision about plans should not be made until a breakthrough in product development occurs.

OR

Plans should not be made until a breakthrough in product development occurs.

EDITOR'S NOTE 8.8 Another form of redundancy is putting two words together that have the same meaning. Since ***definite*** implies something that is a ***decision, future*** implies ***plans***, and ***major*** implies a ***breakthrough,*** the writer can easily cut this phrase in half by simply saying ***decision, plans*** and ***breakthrough;*** more examples are provided in Unit Six of <u>An Editing Workbook for Chinese Technical Writers.</u>

12. ~~It is well known that~~ telecommunications technologies ~~happen to be~~ are expanding rapidly ~~for the purpose of~~ to satisfying the growing consumer demand.

Telecommunications technologies are expanding rapidly to satisfy the growing consumer demand.

Exercise 28

Correct the following sentences using the proofreading marks on page 1.

1. The message is received by the user that subscription to the on-line

    service must be made by the account holder.

2. Confirmation of the data accuracy is required by the quality engineer

    so that customer satisfaction is ensured.

3. The production manager receives information from headquarters that

    evaluation of the finished products must be made by the quality

    inspector.

4. Adjustment of the parameters is unnecessary by the control engineer.

5. A significant decline in the investment return occurred.

6. Significant enhancement of conventional procedures by the proposed

    scheme is possible through the close monitoring of current conditions.

7. The investigator made the suggestion that there is a close relation between the two conditions.

8. The committee came to the conclusion that it is crucial to perform an on-line assessment.

9. There is a necessity for a compromise on the proposal by both parties.

10. There is no need for sole implementation of the environmental awareness program to be the responsibility of the organizing committee.

11. The committee is in a position to make sure that the program is capable of being promulgated successfully.

12. It is our opinion that the current system is deficient of an initial prototype.

Answers

Exercise 28

1. The message is received by the user that subscription to the on-line service must be made by the account holder.

The user receives the message that the account holder must subscribe to the on-line service.

> *EDITOR'S NOTE 8.9* Putting the sentence in active voice not only saves space and makes the sentence more direct, but also places the most important noun at the beginning of the sentence.

2. Confirmation of the data accuracy is required by the quality engineer so that customer satisfaction is ensured.

The quality engineer must confirm the data accuracy to ensure customer satisfaction.

> *EDITOR'S NOTE 8.10* Again, making nouns into verbs and switching to active voice greatly simplify a sentence.

3. The production manager receives information from headquarters that evaluation of the finished products must be made by the quality inspector.

Headquarters informs the production manager that the quality inspector must evaluate the finished products.

4. Adjustment of the parameters is unnecessary by the control engineer.

The control engineer does not need to adjust the parameters.

> **EDITOR'S NOTE 8.11** In the revised sentence the verb ("adjust")hidden inside of the noun ("adjustment") is used by switching from passive voice to active voice.

5. A significant decline in the investment return occurred.

The investment return significantly declined.

6. Significant enhancement of conventional procedures by the proposed scheme is possible through the close monitoring of current conditions.

The proposed scheme can significantly enhance conventional procedures by closely monitoring current conditions.

> **EDITOR'S NOTE 8.12** Turning nouns into verbs makes the sentence less wordy and more direct.

7. The investigator made the suggestion that there is a close relation between the two conditions.

The investigator suggested that the two conditions are closely related.

8. The committee came to the conclusion that it is crucial to perform an on-line assessment.

The committee concluded that an on-line assessment must be performed.

9.   There is a necessity for a compromise on the proposal by both parties.

Both parties must compromise on the proposal.

10. There is no need for implementation of the environmental awareness

program to be the sole responsibility of the organizing committee.

**The organizing committee does not need to be solely responsible for imple-
menting the environmental awareness program.**

11. The committee is in a position to make sure that the program is

capable of being promulgated successfully.

**The committee can make sure that the program can be promulgated
successfully.**

> **EDITOR'S NOTE 8.13** Avoid wordiness by saying **ensure** or **assure** instead of **make sure** when the Chinese meaning is 確定.

12. It is our opinion that the current system is deficient of an initial

prototype.

We believe that the current system lacks a prototype.

Overcoming Chinese-English Colloquial Habits in Writing

(as appeared in the Internet TESL Journal (Japan), Vol. VI, No. 2 February 2000)

Ted Knoy

tedaknoy@ms11.hinet.net

http://mx.nthu.edu.tw/~tedknoy

National Tsing Hua University (Taiwan)

This article introduces common Chinese-English colloquial habits in writing and provides suggestions for instructors concerned with the writing needs of their students. Despite the increasing number of Chinese authors submitting articles to international journals, the colloquial obstacles are seldom addressed. In addition, although an increasing number of on-line writing centers cater to the needs of non-native English speakers, the materials and services provided rarely pinpoint the language-related stumbling blocks that Chinese authors face. Directly translating from Chinese into English is not necessarily grammatically incorrect. Once aware of repetitive writing tendencies, the Chinese writer will begin to realize that directly translating from Chinese can sometimes mask the intended meaning.

Introduction

An increasing number of Chinese authors are submitting articles in English, as evidenced by the growing number of engineering and science colleges in Chinese speaking universities that require doctoral and even master candidates to publish in international journals. However, limited resources are available for helping Chinese authors proofread, edit and prepare their manuscripts for publication. Moreover, in addition to grammatical and writing style errors, Chinese-English colloquial habits often prevent Chinese authors from concisely expressing their intended meaning. Although an increasing number of on-line writing centers cater to the needs of non-native English speaking writers, the materials and services provided rarely pinpoint the language-related stumbling blocks that Chinese authors face when writing. This article summarizes efforts underway at the Chinese On-line Writing Lab (OWL), National Tsing Hua University to incorporate awareness of Chinese-English colloquial habits in the tutorial process.

The Chinese On-line Writing Lab

Originally established in 1989 as University Editing before going on-line in 1997, The Chinese On-line Writing Lab (OWL) at National Tsing Hua University, Taiwan provides comprehensive on-line writing services and learning curricula for Chinese authors of English manuscripts. (URL address: http://mx.nthu.edu.tw/~tedknoy) Staffed by native English speakers who are fluent in Chinese and long term residents of Taiwan, the Chinese OWL stresses the correction of Chinese-English colloquial habits in writing in addition to general writing style and grammatical errors. To achieve this objective, the Chinese OWL has published four books that are part of The Chinese Technical Writers Series. These books concentrate on aiding Chinese technical writers in the following areas: (a) writing (b) structure and content and (c) quality.

Writing in a Non-Native English Speaking Environment

From the perspective of a Chinese writer in a non-native English speaking environment, instead of emulating the writing of a native English speaker, the nature of Chinese-English should be the initial concern. Several helpful books are available on general ESL approaches to writing. However, few of them focus on the unique situation of a Chinese writer in a non-native English speaking environment. As an alternative approach, the language tutor can make the Chinese writer aware of incorrect colloquial habits (separate from writing style and grammatical errors) so that examining alternative ways of constructing sentences slowly begin. This gradual process of experimenting with different ways of constructing sentences in a clear and direct manner is prefered over the copying of words and phrases from international journals. In sum, a writing approach for Chinese students in a non-native English speaking environment should be presented in a Chinese cultural perspective. Such an approach begins with examining the nature of those problems encountered when directly transposing a sentence from Chinese to English.

Tutorial Writing Suggestions for Chinese Writers

The following suggestions for tutorial writing can help both the language instructor and tutor in making the Chinese writer aware of incorrect colloquial habits that occur during composition.

1. Maintain a direct English conversational flow in your manuscript - while maintaining the logical approach of the manuscript - by preventing overuse of traditional textbook words or phrases.

Writing English in a non-English speaking environment can be a formidable task for a Chinese writer. Traditional writing approaches taught in Taiwan (and other Chinese speaking countries) have sometimes placed an unrealistic demand on the Chinese writer to produce compositions of the same quality as those of native English speakers. While this does not mean that experienced Chinese writers can not produce excellent English manuscripts, such an expectation placed on the Chinese graduate student or novice writer trying to publish in English for the first time is unrealistic. Although foreign journals and publications provide valuable references, traditional teaching styles have frequently over emphasized the need to emulate them. Another problem created by relying too heavily on foreign journals and publications is that the writer can often not justify why a sentence has been written in a particular manner. This can lead to plagarism and is therefore not recommended. Also, this approach of writing is dangerous due to the lack of standardized technical writing curriculum in Taiwan universities and research institutions. Both unrealistic quality expectations and the overemphasis on sentence phrases and structures taken from foreign journals and publications as a writing source have unfortunately led towards random copying and sometimes, even plagiarism.

2. Place the most important subject and/or clause at the beginning of the sentence so as to make the primary idea or emphasis more accessible.

Why is the main idea or primary emphasis occasionally unclear in English sentences written by Chinese authors? The primary emphasis or key idea of a sentence is often lost when directly translating from spoken/written Chinese and over relying on use of traditional textbook words or phrases occurs. Often the intended meaning is hidden within the sentence. Unless the intention is to connect with the previous sentence, this tendency robs the manuscript of a direct English conversational flow that, in contrast, often places the primary emphasis or key idea at the beginning of the sentence.

3. Avoid the over used tendency of placing prepositional and other phrases which indicate time (or even adverbs which indicate time) at the beginning of the sentence.

The Chinese verb form does not have a well defined past, present or future tense. In writing or in speaking, the tense of the Chinese verb is unclear. Therefore, when Chinese is used, prepositional or other phrases (as well as conjunctive adverbs) which indicate time, are placed at the beginning of a sentence so as to inform the speaker or the reader of the appropriate tense. When translating into English, Chinese writers occasionally forget that English has a well-defined past/present/future verb tense. Consequently, the unconscious tendency is often redundant. Consider the following example of this Chinese-English colloquial habit: Now, the company is planning to expand production. Emphasizing Now at the beginning of the sentence is only redundant since the sentence is already in present tense.

4. Avoid the over used tendency of placing prepositional and other phrases that indicate

comparison at the beginning of the sentence.

Chinese writers often place prepositional phrases that indicate comparison in front of the main idea. That which the main idea is being compared to (not the idea itself) is often placed at the beginning of the sentence. In doing so, the main idea is pushed towards the end of the sentence. Consider the following example of this Chinese-English colloquial habit: ***Compared to dogs, cats are nice.*** Instead, one should say ***Cats are nicer than dogs***.

5. Avoid constant prefacing of the main idea by stating the purpose, condition, location or reason first.

Chinese writers often preface the main idea by first stating the purpose, condition, location or reason. The logic behind this colloquial habit is that by introducing or directly stating the main idea would be too direct and potentially offensive. However, such an introduction before every main idea (or prefacing the fact) may leave the reader with the impression that the author is indirect, as this tendency pushes the main idea towards the end of the sentence. Consider the following example of this Chinese-English colloquial habit, where sentences often begin with: purpose (***In order to*** and ***For the sake of***) condition (***If*** and ***When***) location (***In***, ***At***, and ***From***) or reason (***Due to***, ***Because***, and ***Since***).

6. Use transitional phrases to connect two sentences or two paragraphs.

Although placing the main idea towards the beginning of a sentence is a good idea, always doing so would confine the sentence so the paper seems to lack any connection between sentences and paragraphs. To connect sentences, Chinese writers often rely on conjunctive adverbs (e.g. Thus, Therefore, Consequently, and So). Additionally, the Chinese writer must place prepositional and other phrases that indicate transition at the beginning of a sentence. A transitional effect is desired when attempting to make a connection with the previous sentence or paragraph. A balance between placing the most important emphasis at the beginning of a sentence, along with occasionally creating a transitional effect, allows the Chinese writer to directly and smoothly express the desired content.

7. Avoid long sentences by limiting each sentence to preferably one or two primary ideas and using semi-colons.

English sentences by Chinese writers are often too long and sometimes appear awkward in that the main idea is often lost. This is puzzling as Chinese often stresses the clarity, wholeness of thought being expressed and contained in one sentence. Recall point #5 where prefaces that denote purpose, reason, location and reason are often added before the main idea as a form of introduction. Adding a preface at the beginning of each sentence obviously lengthens the sentence. When translating into English, many Chinese writers are often afraid of separate a sentence between the main and supporting clause because it is thought that by dividing the main idea into two sentences, the reader my not see the connection in the formation of a complete idea. The result is a long, awkward sentence. An alternative method is the use of a semi-colon, seldom used among Chinese technical writers.

8. Prevent overuse of First Person; Third Person is more objective.

First Person is so common in Chinese documents (professional or otherwise) that many writers are unaware of this colloquial habit. The writer tends to lose objectivity in the manuscript with overusing First Person; in addition, the main idea becomes lost in the sentence. Emphasis of a personal opinion such as *We believe*, *We can infer*, *We conclude*, *We recommend*, and *We postulate*, however, can be used. In contrast, using the Third Person removes a feeling of subjectivity or personal bias that the First Person style has. Moreover, Third Person creates an objective environment so as to allow the readers to assess the quality of the manuscript.

Conclusion

From the perspective of language tutors at the Chinese On-line Writing Lab (OWL), National Tsing Hua University, Taiwan and while focusing on the unique situation of a Chinese writer in a non-native English speaking environment, the Chinese OWL advocates an alternative approach. That is, the tutor points out incorrect colloquial habits (separate from writing style and grammatical errors). In doing so, the writer slowly begins to examine alternate sentence constructions rather than using conventional formations. Moreover, the suggested tutorial writing provides a valuable reference for on-line writing labs concerned with this growing segment of writers.

References

Knoy, Ted (1993). <u>An English Style Approach for Chinese Technical Writers</u>. Taipei, Taiwan: Hua Hsiang Yuan

Knoy, Ted (2000). <u>An Editing Workbook for Chinese Technical Writers</u>. Hsinchu, Taiwan: C Web Technology

About the Author

Born on his father's birthday, (September 20, 1965), Ted Knoy received a Bachelor of Arts in History at Franklin College of Indiana (Franklin, Indiana) and a Masters of Public Administration at American International College (Springfield, Massachusetts). Having conducted research and independent study in South Africa, India, Nicaragua, and Switzerland, he has lived in Taiwan since 1989 where he is a permanent resident. He is currently reading for a Ph.d in Education at the University of Leicester (U. K.).

An associate researcher at Union Chemical Laboratories (Industrial Technology Research Institute), Ted is also a technical writing instructor at the Department of Computer Science, National Tsing Hua University as well as the Institute for Information Management and the Department of Communications Engineering, National Chiao Tung University. He is also the English editor of several technical and medical journals in Taiwan.

Ted is author of the Chinese Technical Writers Series, which includes An English Style Approach for Chinese Technical Writers, English Oral Presentations for Chinese Technical Writers, A Correspondence Manual for Chinese Technical Writers, An Editing Workbook for Chinese Technical Writers, and Advanced Copyediting Practice for Chinese Technical Writers.

Ted created and coordinates the Chinese OWL (On-line Writing Lab) at http://mx.nthu.edu.tw/~tedknoy

Acknowledgments

Professors Su Chao-Ton and Tong Lee-Eeng of the Department of Industrial Management at National Chiao Tung University are appreciated for the use of their materials. Tamara Reynish and Scott Vokey are also appreciated for reviewing this Workbook.

精通科技論文(報告)寫作之捷徑

An English Style Approach For Chinese Technical Writers　　（修訂版）

作者：柯泰德（Ted Knoy）

內容簡介

使用直接而流利的英文會話
讓您所寫的英文科技論文很容易被了解
提供不同形式的句型供您參考利用
比較中英句子結構之異同
利用介系詞片語將二個句子連接在一起

萬其超／李國鼎科技發展基金會秘書長

本書是多年實務經驗和專注力之結晶，因此是一本坊間少見而極具實用價值的書。

陳文華／國立清華大學工學院院長

中國人使用英文寫作時，語法上常會犯錯，本書提供了很好的實例示範，對於科技論文寫作有相當參考價值。

徐　章／工業技術研究院量測中心主任

這是一個讓初學英文寫作的人，能夠先由不犯寫作的錯誤開始再根據書中的步驟逐步學習提升寫作能力的好工具，　此書的內容及解說方式使讀者也可以無師自通，藉由自修的方式學習進步，但是更重要的是它雖然是一本好書，當您學會了書中的許多技巧，如果您還想要更進步，那麼基本原則還是要常常練習，才能發揮書中的精髓。

Kathleen Ford, English Editor, Proceedings(Life Science Divison),
National Science Council

The Chinese Technical Writers Series is valuable for anyone involved with creating scientific documentation.

特　　價　　新台幣 300 元
發 行 所　　華香園出版社　印行

作好英語會議簡報

English Oral Presentations for Chinese Technical Writers

A Case Study Approach

作者：柯泰德（Ted Knoy）

內容簡介

本書共分十二個單元，涵括產品開發、組織、部門、科技、及產業的介紹、科技背景、公司訪問、研究能力及論文之發表等，每一單元提供不同型態的科技口頭簡報範例，以進行英文口頭簡報的寫作及表達練習，是一本非常實用的著作。

李鍾熙 / 工業技術研究院化學工業研究所所長

一個成功的科技簡報，就是使演講流暢，用簡單直接的方法、清楚表達內容。本書提供一個創新的方法(途徑)，給組織每一成員做為借鏡，得以自行準備口頭簡報。利用本書這套有系統的方法加以練習，將必然使您信心備增，簡報更加順利成功。

薛敬和 / IUPAC 台北國際高分子研討會執行長
國立清華大學教授

本書以個案方式介紹各英文會議簡之執行方式，深入簡出，為邁入實用狀況的最佳參考書籍。

沙晉康 / 清華大學化學研究所所長
第十五屆國際雜環化學會議主席

本書介紹英文簡報的格式，值得國人參考。今天在學術或工商界與外國接觸來往均日益增多，我們應加強表達的技巧，尤其是英文的簡報應具有很高的專業手準。本書做為一個很好的範例。

張俊彥 / 國立交通大學電機資訊學院教授兼院長

針對中國學生協助他們寫好英文的國際論文和參加國際會議如何以英語演講、內容切中要害特別推薦。

| 特　　　價 | 新台幣 250 元 |
| 發 行 所 | 揚智出版社　印行 |

科技英文寫作系列之三

英文信函參考手冊

A Correspondence Manual for Chinese Technical Writers

作者： 柯泰德 （Ted Knoy）

內容簡介

本書期望成爲從事專業管理與科技之中國人，在國際場合上溝通交流時之參考指導書籍。本書所提供的書信範例（ 附磁碟片），可爲您撰述信件時的參考範本。更實際的是，本書如同一「寫作計畫小組」，能因應特定場合（ 狀況 ） 撰寫出所需要的信函。

李國鼎 / 總統府資政

我國科技人員在國際場合溝通表達之機會急遽增加，希望大家都來重視英文說寫之能力。

羅明哲 / 國立中興大學教務長

一份表達精準且適切的英文信函，在國際間的往來交流上，重要性不亞於研究成果的報告發表。本書介紹各類英文技術信函的特徵及寫作指引，所附範例中肯實用，爲優良的學習及參考書籍。

廖俊臣 / 國立清華大學理學院院長

本書提供許多有關工業技術合作、技術轉移 、工業資訊 、人員訓練及互訪等接洽信函的例句和範例，頗爲實用，極具參考價值。

于樹偉 / 工業安全衛生技術發展中心主任

國際間往來日益頻繁，以英文有效地溝通交流，是現今從事科技研究人員所需具備的重要技能。本書在寫作風格、文法結構與取材等方面，提供極佳的寫作參考與指引，所列舉的範例，皆經過作者細心的修訂與潤飾，必能切合讀者的實際需要。

特　　價　　新台幣 250 元

發 行 所　　揚智出版社　印行

科技英文編修訓練手冊

An Editing Workbook For Chinese Technical Writers

作者: 柯泰德 (Ted Knoy)

內容簡介

要把科技英文寫的精確並不是件容易的事情。通常在投寄文稿發表前,作者都要前前後後修改草稿,在這樣繁複過程中甚至最後可能請專業的文件編修人士代勞雕琢使全文更爲清楚明確。

本書由科技論文的寫作型式、方法型式、內容結構及內容品質著手,並以習題方式使學生透過反覆練習熟能生巧,能確實提昇科技英文之寫作及編修能力。

劉炯朗 / 國立清華大學校長

「科技英文寫作」式一項非常重要的技巧。本書針對台灣科技研究人員在英文寫作發表這方面的訓練,書中以實用性練習對症下藥,期望科技英文寫作者熟能生巧,實在是一個很有用的教材。

彭旭明 / 國立台灣大學副校長

本書爲科技英文寫作系列之四;以練習題爲主,由反覆練習中提昇寫作及編輯能力。適合理、工、醫、農的學生及研究人員使用,特爲推薦。

許千樹 / 國立交通大學研究發展處研發長

處於今日高科技時代,國人用到科技英文寫作之機會甚多,如何能以精練的手法寫出一篇好的科技論文,極爲重要。本書針對國人寫作之缺點提供了各種清楚的編修範例,實用性高,極具參考價值。

陳文村 / 國立清華大學電機資訊學院院長

處在我國日益國際化、資訊化的社會裡,英文書寫是必備的能力,本書提供很多極具參考價值的範例。柯泰德先生在清大任敎科技英文寫作多年,深受學生喜愛,本人樂於推薦此書。

特　　價	新台幣 350 元	
劃　　撥	19419482	清蔚科技股份有限公司
線上訂購	四方書網	www.4Book.com.tw
發 行 所	清蔚科技	印行

The Chinese On-line Writing Lab OWL

柯泰德線上英文論文編修訓練服務

http://mx.nthu.edu.tw/~tedknoy

您有科技英文寫作上的困擾嗎？

您的文章在投稿時常被國外論文審核人員批評文法很爛嗎？以至於被退稿嗎？

您對論文段落的時式使用上常混淆不清嗎？

您在寫作論文時同一個動詞或名詞常常重複使用嗎？

您的這些煩惱現在均可透過*柯泰德網路線上科技英文論文編修服務*
來替您加以解決。本服務項目分別含括如下：

1. 英文論文編輯與修改
2. 科技英文寫作開課訓練服務
3. 線上寫作家教
4. 免費寫作格式建議服務，及網頁問題討論區解答

另外，為能廣為服務中國人士對論文寫作上之缺點，柯泰德先生亦同
時著作下列參考書籍可供有志人士作為寫作上之參考。

〈1. 精通科技論文(報告)寫作之捷徑
〈2. 做好英文會議簡報
〈3. 英文信函參考手冊
〈4. 科技英文編修訓練手冊
〈5. 有效撰寫英文讀書計畫

上部份亦可由柯泰德先生的首頁中下載得到。

如果您對本服務有興趣的話，可參考柯泰德先生的首頁展示。

柯泰德網路線上科技英文論文編修服務

地址：新竹市大學路50號8樓之三
TEL:03-5724895
FAX:03-5724938
網址：http://mx.nthu.edu.tw/~tedknoy
E-mail:tedaknoy@ms11.hinet.net

備註：您若有英文論文需要柯先生修改，請直接將文件以電子郵寄(E-mail)的
方式，寄至上面地址，建議以WORD存檔；您也可以把存有您文件的小磁碟片
(1.44MB規格)以一般郵政的方式寄達。不論您採用那種方式，都請註明您的大
名及聯絡電話，以及所選文件修改的速度(5日內或10日內完成)。有任何問
題，請隨時來電，謝謝。

國家圖書館出版品預行編目資料

科技英文編修手冊 - 進階篇 / 柯泰德(Ted Knoy)作　—初版—

新竹市：清蔚科技，2000【民89】

面；21x29.7公分(科技英文寫作系列；5)

譯自：Advanced Copyediting Practice for Chinese Technical Writers

ISBN　957-97544-2-X　　(平裝)

1.英國語言 - 寫作法　2.論文寫作法

805.17　　　　　　　　　　　　　　　　　　89008721

科技英文寫作系列五

科技英文編修訓練手冊 - 進階篇

作　　　者／柯泰德(Ted Knoy)

發　行　人／徐明哲

法律顧問／志揚國際法律事務所

發　行　所／清蔚科技股份有限公司

網　　　址／http://www.CWeb.com.tw

電子郵件／Comment@Cweb.com.tw

地　　　址／新竹市300國立清華大學創新育成中心301室

電　　　話／03-574-1020

傳　　　眞／03-574-1021

印　刷　所／馨視覺編印中心

美工設計／陳偉婷

打字排版／陳偉婷

版　　　次／2000年8月 初版　2003年2月二刷

國際書碼／ISBN 957-97544-2-X

建議售價／450元

劃撥帳號／帳戶　清蔚科技股份有限公司

　　　　　　帳號　19419482

四方書網 http://www.4Book.com.tw